Sedona Sunset

Tanya Stowe

Sedona Sunset

COPYRIGHT 2014 by Tanya Stowe

Contact Information: titleadmin@pelicanbookgroup.com

Cover Art *by Nicola Martinez*

White Rose Publishing, a division of Pelican Ventures, LLC
www.pelicanbookgroup.com PO Box 1738 *Aztec, NM * 87410

White Rose Publishing Circle and Rosebud logo is a trademark of Pelican Ventures, LLC

Publishing History
First White Rose Edition, 2015
Paperback Edition ISBN 978-1-61116-420-6
Electronic Edition ISBN 978-1-61116-419-0
Published in the United States of America

Dedication

For my dad, who first introduced me to the wonders of
Arizona.

Praise

A Cowboy Christmas:

Fans of good clean reads will certainly enjoy this book, a feel-good story that left me wanting to read more from these authors! ~ Brenda Casto

Lea's Gift:

Lea's Gift would be a perfect [movie, a] Christmas tradition to watch year after year after year. ~ Trudi Loprieto

1

Beautiful. Breathtaking. Lara Fallon stopped on the flagstone walkway to watch the most spectacular sunset she'd ever seen. "Brett," she whispered. "Do you see this? Isn't it incredible?"

Her father's right-hand man and her best friend paused on the path from the guesthouse to the main house and glanced up.

"It's just a sunset, Lara, it happens every day."

But not like this. Not in a burst of brilliant, burnt orange that lit every cloud for hundreds of miles. Not with a halo of golden rays spilling into the canyon to pierce every dark corner. The shifting angle of the light had changed the very feel and texture of the air. Everything looked softer, gentler, golden.

Lara took a slow, deep breath, inhaling the curiously mixed scent of dry earth and pines. This morning when she'd left New York, she'd looked up at a cold, pewter sky and nearly slipped on a patch of January ice. Now she stood on a mountain path, wearing a pale blue evening gown and marveling at the spectacle of an Arizona sky.

The tension inside her spun away like an untethered web caught in a soft breeze. The red rocks of Sedona were said to possess mystical, healing powers. Right now, Lara believed it.

Brett had proceeded ahead of her. Now he came back around a bend in the path, his features twisted

1

into a tight frown. "Lara, I promised Troy I'd be early to help greet the guests and I'm late."

Sedona's rocks didn't seem to be helping Brett relax. In fact, he was more stressed than Lara had ever seen him. Given the fact that tomorrow was the dedication of the Fallon School of Art and Brett had been working on the project for more than a year, she could understand why he might be tense.

But they'd been separated for six months. Now they were together, and Brett couldn't spare two minutes to stand beside her and watch the sunset. Something was wrong. Definitely wrong.

"Why does Troy need your help? Eliza is his wife and she's one of New York's best-loved hostesses. That's why she and my mother got along so well." Lara sounded almost petulant, more so than she intended.

"Things have been different since they've been here, Lara. Eliza's not herself."

Lara halted. Troy and Eliza were like family to her. Eliza and Lara's daily phone calls had slowed since they'd moved to Sedona for the project, but Lara didn't think they'd drifted that far from each other.

"What do you mean, 'not herself?' Is she ill?"

"No, nothing like that. It's just taken a lot more to build this house than Troy anticipated. Between that and the school, it's been stressful. Things have been a little...strained between them. And then there's Christy. She hasn't taken the move very well."

"No eleven-year-old takes a move well."

"I suppose, but the emotional upheaval and puberty hormones have caused a pretty serious flare-up in Christy's rheumatoid arthritis. Eliza has her hands full dealing with that."

Lara's arms dropped to her sides. "Brett, what in the world is going on? How could all of this be happening and no one, not you, or Liza, or Troy, has mentioned a word of it to me?"

He shrugged, frustrated. "What would be the point? What could you do?"

The words hit Lara and penetrated deep. Her eyes burned with moisture. "I guess you're right." She curled her hair behind one ear, hoping her voice didn't sound quite as tight as she thought it might. "An invalid wouldn't be much help to any of you in stressful times."

Brett blinked.

Lara was just as surprised the words had popped out of her mouth.

"I didn't mean *that*. I meant…" Brett began.

"You didn't mean to say it," she interrupted. "But you were thinking it. Everyone does. Since that's the case, don't you feel we should talked about it? At least you and I should." Was there a silent appeal in her tone? Or anger? She didn't know what she was feeling. She only knew that she'd taken one look at that wildly majestic sunset and suddenly felt different. Transformed. A little wild, herself.

Definitely changed.

Brett ran a hand through his hair, leaving it charmingly disheveled. Poor Brett. The next two days were probably going to be the most important of his career, and three hours after arriving from New York, his best friend had complicated his life with an uncharacteristic emotional outburst.

"I'm sorry." She was, but her tone remained taut. "Jet lag is making me crabby."

Brett shoved his hands in his pockets and glanced

up at her. Once. Twice. "Yeah. I guess it's been a pretty difficult week for us all."

He looked and sounded as unconvinced as Lara, but they were calling a truce. After the official opening ceremonies and festivities, they would sit down and straighten this out. Brett had helped her through the days and months after the accident. Tomorrow, they'd look back at this and laugh.

Lara fell into step behind Brett and they rounded a corner, coming in full view of the three-story pueblo style house. She halted again, struck by the pure, pristine lines of the building.

An artist, Troy's wood sculptures and carvings were some of the finest in the world. His latest creative ambition was to design his dream house.

Lara and her father had wondered if he would be able to transfer his incredible ideas into a reality. First appearances said yes.

The structure was deep amber, the color of the Sedona rocks, and multilevel with entire walls made of tinted glass. It looked like some modernistic dwelling tucked into the wall of the Sedona canyon, a colored jewel in a dark brown setting. It fit so perfectly, as if had always been there. All the lines had a purity of vision that somehow fell into the natural landscape. The house was a Southwest castle.

Lara was impressed. If the inside was half as tastefully done as the exterior, Troy had outdone himself.

She took a step forward and for the first time noticed a man at the corner of the house. Standing deep in the shadows beneath a full-grown scrub oak, he was almost invisible. He wore sunglasses and was dressed in black from head to toe. He lifted a hand to his ear and said something in a low, curt voice. A black cord looped over his ear.

Brett came back, every move betraying his impatience. When he saw where her gaze was directed, he sighed.

"The insurance company insisted Troy hire additional security. They felt his own high tech, extremely expensive system wouldn't be enough to protect La Guitarra."

Brett took her arm and gently guided her toward the entrance. "Troy wasn't satisfied with filling his house with priceless Indian and Spanish-Colonial antiquities. He had to have something else, something spectacular and memorable to showcase for the opening. So he brought in a three-hundred-year-old gypsy guitar complete with its own legend of lost lovers. I'm surprised you don't know about it. It's one of the oldest survivors of its kind. Your father knew of it."

Lara stiffened. "Why are you surprised? You know my father never talks about his business with me."

It was Brett's turn to pause. "Well, that's true, of course. But you always had a grasp of what went on."

A brittle laugh escaped Lara. "Only because you're his right-hand man and you talked. Now that you're here in Sedona, I'm completely out of the loop."

The troubled look on Brett's face made her feel guilty. Sighing, she placed her hand over his. "I didn't mean that to sound quite so bitter. It doesn't hurt that Father excludes me from the business. I've gotten over that. In fact, keeping up with all of Fallon Enterprises can be exhausting. I've actually enjoyed these last six months off. It's given me time to do a lot of thinking."

Instead of easing Brett's discomfort, her words

seemed to agitate him more. He hesitated, as if he wanted to say something, but they'd reached the double doors of the house. Sealing his lips into a tight line, he led her through the wide, tiled entry.

Hanging from the multi-level ceiling, an exquisite filigree candelabra made of rust-colored iron glowed with candle-shaped, flickering lights. To their right, an iron balustrade in the same delicate filigree pattern ran up a curving staircase and disappeared.

Lara had just enough time to catch an impression of cool, comforting earth tone colors...amber, beige, burnt orange, dark wood.

Then Troy came toward her, his hands extended. Like Brett, he dressed in a tux. For a man over fifty, he looked incredibly young and terribly handsome.

He gave her a light hug that paid homage to her expensive dress and artfully done hair. Troy was the consummate gentleman. Then he held her at arm's length to look at her.

Lara grew uncomfortable, certain that when Troy viewed her, he saw her mother's fine-boned form, honey-blonde hair, and delicate features.

"Lara," he said with a warm smile. "You look...stunning."

The pause set Lara off. It allowed the doubts to creep in. In everyone's mind, she was still poor, little Lara. The attitude irritated her. "You mean healthy, don't you?"

Troy hesitated. "No, I mean stunning. Vibrant. Beautiful. Stunning." His words were sincere. He meant it.

Lara was sure of it, but once the doubts had started, she couldn't seem to stop them. "Like my mother?" she asked.

Troy's hands fell away from her arms.

Lara caught her lip. What was wrong with her? These people were family to her. After the accident that had killed her mother and nearly crippled her, Lara had asked over and over why God had taken her mother and left her.

Troy had been one of the bulwarks. He'd pulled her through with his conviction that God loved all his children equally.

When Troy, Eliza, and Brett left New York, Lara had felt bereft, and abandoned. She struggled to get through the six-month separation. Now they were all together again, and she seemed determined to pick a fight with someone...anyone. What was wrong with her?

Brett stepped into the awkward silence. "Lara's had a long day, Troy. She's feeling a little edgy."

"Of course, of course. Perfectly understandable." Troy leaned forward to kiss Lara's forehead.

She let him. But her stomach churned again.

Reliable, dependable Brett. She could always count on him to back her up, to forgive her and to make concessions for her "condition." The problem was she didn't have a condition. Not anymore. She wasn't overtired, worn down, or edgy and she didn't want anyone making excuses for her.

Eliza called her name and hurried toward her.

With relief, Lara pulled away from the men.

In her mid-thirties, petite and almost too slender, with a mass of long, curly red hair that refused to be tamed, Eliza looked spectacular. She wore a flowing, floor-length gown of brilliant multi-colored silk patterned with midsized flowers in fall colors. Burnt orange, gold, and burgundy blended in and over each other, as bright as the sunset. On Eliza, it looked elegant, tasteful, and vibrant.

She grabbed Lara in a fierce hug, completely ignoring her gown and perfectly styled hair.

Lara's eyes misted with glad tears. It was wonderful to see her friend.

"Heavens, you look great!" Eliza exclaimed. "What have you been doing to yourself while we've been gone?"

"Same old, same old." Lara brushed over the compliment. "But Brett tells me things haven't been so good with you." Now that she was closer, she could see the violet smudges beneath Eliza's eyes. They were artfully hidden by makeup, but to someone who knew Eliza well, they told their own tale.

"Sometimes Brett cares too much," Eliza said. "There's nothing wrong that can't be fixed, especially now that you're here."

"Now that I'm here?" Lara repeated in disbelief. A moment ago she'd been made to feel like a useless invalid. In half a breath, Eliza had her feeling valuable. With a laugh of sheer pleasure, she grabbed the other woman in another hug. "I've missed you so much," she murmured. "Tell me what you need. I'm sure I won't be as much help as you think, but I'll do whatever you want."

"Did you bring your ballet shoes?" Eliza asked.

"Of course, I dance every day. It's my therapy."

Behind them, the door opened. Eliza stood on her tiptoes to peer over Lara's taller, five foot eight inch frame. "There's Rupert Townsend. He hasn't dropped a dime for the school. Troy needs me to schmooze him. There'll be no time to talk tonight, but tomorrow, after the dedication ceremonies, meet me here and bring your shoes. I'll give you the grand tour of this monstrosity and explain everything." Pressing a quick kiss to her cheek, Eliza hurried around her.

Lara turned to watch her friend greet grumpy, old man Townsend.

Beside Eliza, Troy's gaze never left his wife as she turned on her charm. A slow, soft smile slipped over his lips and his hand came to rest on the small of her back. It was a loving, possessive gesture Lara had seen time and again between the two. Things couldn't be all that wrong if Troy could still look at Eliza like that.

Lara felt better just seeing it.

Standing beside Lara, Brett also witnessed the intimate gesture and it seemed to make him uncomfortable. He pulled at his shirt collar, and then ducked his head and stuffed his hands in his pockets. His glance strayed toward Lara and their gazes met. She waited, hoping he would hold out his hand, hoping he would tell her what troubled him.

Brett and Lara had an understanding. Lara needed to recover and Brett had been consumed with work on the school. But once past those times, they would explore their friendship more, maybe move into a deeper type of relationship.

Lara was ready for that, ready for the same kind of intimacy they'd just witnessed. She hoped Brett was ready, too.

Instead, his hands stayed in his pockets and he stared across the empty space.

After a few moments, Lara walked in the opposite direction.

Brett followed, but someone called his name and he turned away.

Rooms passed by in a blur of earth tones and

contrasting dark woods. Ahead of Lara, French doors led to a balcony. She headed for them and slipped outside. The air had cooled just since they'd gone inside. The sun had lost its grip on the world and dusk was fast on its heels. Lara leaned forward on the stucco wall that formed the edge of the balcony. Its rough texture bit into her hands, and she welcomed it.

Odd. Brett's lack of attention made her angry, not hurt. He'd been focused on the school for ages. She'd been patient and dutiful, waiting for this week, making plans and envisioning how it would be when they were together at last.

The school had been her mother's dream. After her death, her father had begun the work as a way to deal with his grief. He'd assigned the project to Brett, and the school progressed at the same pace as Lara's recovery. The two had joined in her mind. Now the school was finished and Lara healed. She had come to these ceremonies determined to see the school and her new life launched. She'd waited a long time to start her over, but things weren't going as planned.

She glanced up to catch the last flashes of the setting sun. At least she wouldn't miss the sunset. Even if she had to see it alone, it was worth it.

The sun, a brilliant orange ball, sat on the crest of the canyon, half gone, trying desperately to send last vestiges of color into the darkening sky.

Lara walked along the balcony that ran the length of the house, following as the bright circle sank behind the mountain. Its last rays caught the clouds and lit the sky in an explosion of orange and gold before it finally disappeared.

Lara turned toward the house. Farther down the balcony, a man leaned against the low retaining wall with both hands. He was tall, with a dark complexion accented by a loose, full-sleeved white shirt. Longish hair hung just over his ears. Something about him intrigued Lara.

European. He looked European. Experience was written in the lines of his face. He had a strong, straight nose and full, well-shaped lips. A broad, strong brow made his brown eyes look hooded. He turned toward her, and the wind ruffled his dark hair. A slight frown creased his forehead, making his gaze seem intense, focused on her.

Lara shivered. Rubbing her hands along her arms, she turned and moved back inside. But she took the wrong set of French doors. This pair led into a small sitting area off the formal living room. Across from Lara, poised on a table, was La Guitarra.

Lara's father had made his fortune in antiques. She'd grown up around the family business so she recognized a fine piece when she saw it. She moved closer, studying the unusual instrument. Even if Brett hadn't told her something about La Guitarra, she would have known it had a past. The aged wood spoke of a well-loved instrument.

It would be unthinkable to add the oils of her hands to the guitar's unfinished wooden surface. If Brett followed procedure—which he always did—the stand would be mounted on a sensor. Any lessening or adding of weight and alarms would ring throughout the house. But still, looking at the guitar's dark surface, polished only by the touch of its players, her hand involuntarily raised.

"Compelling, isn't it?"

Startled, Lara turned.

The man from the balcony stood inside the French

doors, leaning against the jamb with his arms crossed. He must have thought Lara was about to touch the guitar. Embarrassed, she clenched her fingers and lowered her hand.

He motioned to the guitar. "I can never look at it without wanting to touch it," he said.

"I would never—"

"But you wanted to." He pushed away from the door and came toward her.

Lara's stomach jumped.

The way he moved, loose-limbed and smooth, powerful. Almost predatory.

It made her want to run. She backed up until she felt the table behind her.

He towered over her, almost certainly well over six feet. Up close, his eyes proved strangely light, not brown after all, but a hazel color. A small cleft pierced his chin. His features were not classically handsome, but arresting. And he spoke in pure clean, American tones, without a trace of a European accent.

"La Guitarra begs to be touched," he said, jolting her from her examination. "Like most pieces of art. Its lines are pure, made for the hands." His gaze traced over her shoulders and down one arm and suddenly, she didn't think he spoke of the guitar.

Flustered, she turned toward the instrument. "You seem to know a lot about art, Mr.—"

"Alex. Call me Alex."

His too-familiar tone set her senses jumping and she struggled to harness them. Purposely turning away, she managed a half-haughty tone. "Since you know so much, you should also know that touching destroys some art."

"Ah, but not La Guitarra. It's part of the legend."

She couldn't resist. She had to look at him. When she did, he stepped closer so they were almost touching. She could feel his heat. He smelled of soap and something tart and intriguing. Something memorable she couldn't name.

Reaching across the space, he clasped her shoulders and turned her to face the guitar. He stood behind her, so near his breath moved the hair near the nape of her neck. His voice was low and rich as velvet. "Once, a young man—not a renowned luthier, but a simple peasant named Juan Miguel loved the music of his people," he murmured and then stopped.

In the silence, Lara could hear her own ragged breath. It sounded intimate, sensual. She rushed to cover it with a question. "A luthier?"

"Someone who makes stringed instruments. Juan bought the finest wood and shaped a special guitar, using all the care and passion inside him. When he finished, he took it to an old gypsy woman for a spell. He asked that when he played, people would feel his love of life."

Lara's gaze dropped to the hand resting on her left shoulder. It was warm and lean and strong. The kind of fingers that could coax music from a simple guitar and make a woman feel things she'd never felt before.

"Juan was a vibrant man who loved life and when he played, everyone heard that love. Magic flowed from the guitar and captured all who heard it, including a beautiful young gypsy girl. Lucia could not resist him," he whispered. "Juan played, and she danced. He played so her body moved like he played the guitar. The music and her movements were one. All of Juan's passion could be seen in Lucia's body. To watch them was to experience the magic between them."

Magic. Lara could feel it. Sparks sizzled and jumped. If he moved an inch forward, he would be close enough to kiss.

"Soon Juan and Lucia's fame grew. They played and danced through the famous courts of Spain. Lovely Lucia inevitably attracted the attention of a powerful nobleman. A man could not watch her dance without feeling desire. This nobleman tried to seduce her with money and jewels. When none could lure her away from Juan, the nobleman stole her. One night after a performance, masked men snatched Lucia from Juan's arms and rode away. Juan confronted the nobleman, threatened his life, even appealed to the king and queen, but to no avail. Lucia disappeared.

"Juan vowed never to play again. For the rest of his life, he searched for Lucia. La Guitarra sat untouched, unplayed...but it glowed with gypsy magic, begging to be released. Since that time it has passed through many hands and been played many times but never with the power it once possessed. It is said La Guitarra is searching for the lovers who will release the magic trapped inside." He let her go and stepped back.

Lara blinked.

What had just happened? This stranger had practically seduced her with nothing more than the sound of his voice. Ridiculous. She had to get back in control. "Women must find your story impossible to resist." She turned to face him.

He laughed, low and rich. "If I needed it, I'm sure it would work."

True. This man didn't need a romantic story to seduce women. His unusual brooding features would melt most of them…including her. Suddenly, she felt awkward, obvious. "Why did you tell me this?"

"La Guitarra is magic," he said, his voice soft. "It reaches out to some people. Not everyone feels compelled to touch it as you just did."

"I know the value of rare antiques. It doesn't mean I'm hopelessly romantic."

He smiled. "Romantic? Perhaps not. Passionate? Definitely."

Lara laughed. "Now, there you are most definitely wrong."

"Am I?"

His serious tone made the laughter die inside her.

With his chin, he nodded toward the center of the house where most of the guests were gathered. "This house is full of charming people. Inside are incredible jewels, gowns women would kill for, and if your interests are as true as you say, antiquities to rival any collection. And yet, here you are, alone, on a balcony, watching one of nature's most spectacular creations. A sunset." He shook his head. "Trust me. I know true passion when I see it."

Before Lara could form a denial, his hand slid down her arm and cupped her hand in his. Reaching across the space, he pressed her palm to La Guitarra.

Sensation flowed through Lara. The warmth of his body next to hers, the strength of his fingers, controlling her hand. The pure, silky smooth wood. Lara let her eyes close, and her lips part as he stroked her hand down the smooth curve of the guitar and over the sharp edge.

Then abruptly, he loosened his hold and stepped away.

Lara's eyes flew open.

He cupped her chin and traced his thumb beneath her lower lip, never quite touching it. "Passion." Smiling, he turned and left the room.

Even after he'd gone, Lara could feel his touch. Unclenching her fingers, she shook them slightly. What had just happened?

A sensual, enigmatic man had played her. Like an instrument. He'd touched her, and she'd responded. Lara's face burned with humiliation. She heard the sounds of running feet.

Three men dressed in dark clothing burst into the room.

Brett *had* installed sensor alarms—silent alarms.

The men stood just inside the door, searching the room.

"Miss Fallon?"

Lara recognized the man who spoke.

Mike McGraff belonged to the security agency her father's company used most often.

Embarrassed, she gestured toward the table. "I'm sorry," she murmured. "I slipped on the tile and bumped the table."

The men's gazes darted around the room, unconvinced.

Lara stepped away from the table and the guitar. "I'll get out of the way so you can reset the alarm." Hurrying toward the door, she eased out of the room, straight into the noisy babble of the cocktail party.

2

Alex walked out of La Guitarra's room and into another. A smile lingered on his lips. The past few moments easily qualified as the most pleasurable he'd enjoyed since arriving in Sedona. Until a few minutes ago, he'd considered this trip a waste, but the willowy blonde was intriguing. Her pale, fair features made her seem fragile and delicate. She'd pulled the sides of her hair back behind her ears, but the ends still managed to curl around her face in a coy, shy manner.

Her conservative gown had a straight neck, not even revealing the hollow at the base of her throat. The short sleeves gave away nothing. Everything about her was understated and subdued. But still...

The shimmery blue of her gown caught the blue of her eyes, made them intensely bright. When she moved, the gown's silky texture revealed a shapely curve with a teasing hint of what lay beneath. A slit up the side of the gown, exposed a well formed leg, completely covered with a matching shimmery blue stocking.

Modest, but tantalizing. Shy, but filled with a passionate curiosity for La Guitarra. Few people recognized its unique qualities. She had, and so had Troy Madrigal.

Pausing, Alex looked around the room he'd entered. Troy was an unusual man with distinctive taste. A haven of earth tones, the man's home wore the deep red of the rocks, along with beige and brown hues that pressed against pristine, sandstone walls and arching doorways. Exquisite.

Right now, people were packed into the house. Voices rose and fell in a subdued monotone. Glasses clinked. Polite conversation was broken by occasional laughter. Women in luminous gowns draped over crème colored, overstuffed sofas. In a plush brown side chair, two couples held a private conversation. No one seemed interested in the beauty surrounding them.

That's why Alex preferred not to perform at social gatherings like this. They were designed for one thing…for people to see and be seen. Alex had no time or patience for the attitude. Not much could make him suffer through another one of these social wastelands, not even Troy Madrigal's respect for La Guitarra. He would not be here if UNESCO had not asked him to look into this event.

The UNESCO organization for the protection of cultural properties had received an anonymous tip that Fallon Enterprises was involved in a black market operation. It appeared UNESCO had good reason to be interested…at least in this home filled with South American effigies, Spanish Colonial polygraph carvings, Mexican textiles, even some very old, very distinctive Chaco pottery.

If Alex wasn't mistaken, not far away, set in the recessed wall and glass encased, was a clay water pitcher, a duck effigy in black design on white, probably made around 1100 AD. Alex was no expert on so-called "Anasazi" pottery, but he knew the black on white period pieces were the most valuable.

This was a stunning example. He could see no marks, cracks or breaks. A nine-hundred-year old piece of pottery in perfect condition. It belonged in a museum.

Instead, it was here, in Troy Madrigal's home.

It had to have been collected long before the Antiquities Act of 1906 protected ancient Indian sites and made it illegal to collect artifacts and pottery. Troy must have purchased this piece from a private collection created before the law or...he'd purchased it from the black market. UNESCO was wise to question his sources.

Brett Fraser hurried past Alex, bumping his shoulder and barely remembering to apologize. Fraser headed toward La Guitarra's room.

Alex had been waiting for this. For his own sense of safety, he wanted to gauge the response time of the security team during the gatherings, so he'd placed the little blonde's hand on the guitar and waited for the fireworks. He'd purposely stayed close to make sure she didn't take any blame for the security breach.

Alex wasn't aware that Fraser was on the security link, let alone would be one of the first to respond. Interesting. Why was he involved and not Troy?

Alex was about to intercept Fraser and make it clear he had instigated the alarm when Alex's blonde came out of the room and closed the door. With her back against it, she faced Fraser and said something Alex couldn't hear.

Intrigued, Alex stepped closer, purposely eavesdropping from behind the archway.

"La Guitarra is safe," she said in a low voice. "I tripped the alarm."

Fraser said something. He faced the blonde, with his back to Alex, so Alex could only catch words here and there.

"I slipped," she answered.

Fraser touched her arm, seeming concern.

"No, I'm not overtired. The tiles are slippery and I'm wearing two-inch spiky heels."

Alex glanced down. He'd already seen those spiky heels and how well they set off her tiny feet and her fine, shapely legs, but he didn't mind taking another look.

Fraser never even paused. He continued to talk, saying something about stress.

Alex folded his arms and leaned against the arch. Was Fraser blind or just dead? How could he not look when she'd given him a blatant invitation?

Fraser's statement irritated her. "I'm fine," she murmured, her voice low as she motioned toward the door. "You'd better check in with your watch dogs. They were resetting the alarm when I left."

She opened the door, leaving the man no room to argue, and closed it briskly. When she looked around the room, the mixture of boredom and disgust written on her features reflected Alex's feelings about these events. He'd already formed a kinship with this woman. Her bored expression confirmed their emotional bond. But who was she?

He'd been told Daniel Fallon's daughter was scheduled to arrive today. Could the fragile beauty entranced with the sunset and compelled to touch La Guitarra be Fallon's daughter? It didn't make sense. She was far too sensitive, too real. Why would the daughter of one of the world's most successful businessmen prefer sunsets to a social soiree?

"Are you ready?"

The question came from behind Alex. He refused to jump even though the question and the closeness of the speaker had been designed to startle him into a response. Lately, his assistant Carlos always appeared out of nowhere and moved stealthily. Too stealthily, in Alex's opinion. Carlos's behavior had become a problem. Alex would have to take action if something didn't change.

Maintaining his outward calm, Alex slowly turned. "Haven't you learned yet? I'm always ready."

Carlos didn't seem to appreciate the remark. He spun and marched back through the crowd.

With one last glance at Fallon's daughter, Alex followed.

~*~

Lara took a deep, calming breath. She wouldn't let another scene with Brett upset her. Stress alone had made their reunion stilted. Tomorrow would be better and everything would go as she'd planned. It had to. Her whole life, her future depended on it. Considering how badly things had gone so far, the thought made Lara tremble.

A waiter walked by with a tray of champagne glasses. She took one. As she sipped, she strolled around the room. She knew almost everyone there, how much money they had, how many marriages they'd been through and who had the worst taste in clothing. They had all been a part of her life for as long as she could remember. They'd oohed! and ahhed! over her as she grew from a little girl to a young lady. By her mother's side, she'd heard the most intimate details of their lives, but she couldn't remember a single, solitary, real conversation with one of them.

Brett was right. Something had changed. She

wasn't sure what or how it had happened. She felt oddly vulnerable here with the people she'd known all of her life.

She looked for Troy or Eliza, hoping to find sanctuary with one of them. She walked through one room and into another. Eliza was nowhere to be seen and Troy was deep in discussion with a man Lara didn't know. He had the same European look about him as the man she'd encountered on the balcony, only this man was shorter, with long hair pulled back into a ponytail.

"He's a Spaniard. His name is Carlos Bertoleo."

Lara jumped and turned.

Rupert Townsend, a former suitor of her mother's and a constant thorn in her father's side, was a distinguished-looking older man with a shock of white hair. He held out his hand.

"It's good to see you, Mr. Townsend."

He cupped her hand in both of his and lifted it to his lips. "And you my dear, are a breath of fresh air in an otherwise stale room."

Lara's stomach churned. Easing her hand away, she said, "I look like my mother, Mr. Townsend, but I'm not her."

Townsend laughed. "Indeed, you are not. There was only one of your mother. But I'd still like to get to know you better."

"I would probably bore you."

"I doubt that very seriously, my dear." Turning, he nodded toward Troy and the man. "You must have been very interested in something over there not to hear me approach."

"I'm interested in everything here. We *are* celebrating the opening of my mother's school."

"Balderdash. You're a dutiful daughter. You've been told to appreciate it so you're making every effort."

The truth in his words pierced Lara like an arrow. She was here for the opening out of respect and duty. What would come after was more important to her. Everything she was and could be was tied up in the next few weeks. All she wanted was to get this event over with and go on with her life.

"By the way," he continued. "Where is your overlord of a father? Why did he send you off to face this alone?"

Lara stumbled for words. "He's in England. The courts released a very large estate with some incredible antiques. My father had to take possession of it."

"I know all about the release of the Elder estate, and it didn't require your father's presence. That's what he pays his employees to do. It was just an excuse to stay away. He couldn't face coming here." Townsend's acerbic tone softened slightly. "Though I suppose I don't blame him. This brings back far too many memories."

Sedona had been her mother's favorite place and they'd spent many winters here, holding great entertainments and outings for their friends, including Rupert Townsend.

He cleared his throat. "But it's a shame your father left you to face this by yourself. And you can tell him I said so."

A numb little laugh escaped Lara. "I'm sure I'll say it just like that."

Townsend laughed as well. "What's the matter, little girl...not used to plain talk in the Fallon household?"

Lara gave a slight shake of her head. "Not much is said contrary to what my father likes to hear."

"Good girl," he said with a wink. "I knew you didn't buy it."

"It?"

"The Fallon mystique. The concept that Daniel Fallon is infallible and therefore incontestable. I suspected you had a bit of the rebel in you."

"I'm afraid you just heard the extent of my rebelliousness. And I'm a little startled I let that slip out."

Townsend glanced at Bertoleo, and then back at her. "I think you have more fire than you know. Well, time will tell, won't it?" He studied her for a moment before his gaze shot away. "Bertoleo is a very pretentious musician. He plays Flamenco. Calls it 'the rhythms of life.' His playing is average but he has ambitions, so he's arranged to be Alejandro Summers' assistant."

"Alejandro Summers?"

"A genius at the guitar, or so they say. I'm no judge of such things. But I do know Summers is an interesting man. He made his appearance ten, fifteen years ago as a child prodigy, and then disappeared from the public scene for years."

Lara sipped her champagne. Alejandro Summers. The man on the balcony. Even though he'd given her the name Alex, he had to be the same man.

"He's going to play that exquisite piece of art," she said with certainty.

"You mean La Guitarra? Most assuredly. They say Troy paid him a small fortune to be here. I've been told he teaches at the University in Madrid. I'm not sure I believe it. But then, he is able to drop in and out of the limelight. He must not be very serious about his career," he mused. "Ah well, I suppose his patroness is very rich."

"His patroness?"

"La Comtessa de la Guerra. Much older, but still quite smitten with Alejandro. Of course, they were lovers years ago. There have been others, but he always went back to her, at least until she passed away."

Of course. It all fit. His unusual manner. The loose clothing. His confidence and European style.

Lara'd been around men like him all her life. Sophisticated, artistic charmers, men who broke women's hearts for exercise. Usually, she gave them a wide berth, but this one had managed to sneak up behind her. She should have known better.

"If you ask me," Rupert continued, "It's all nonsense. Perhaps La Guitarra is a fine antique, but I think its mystique is pure drivel. Of course, I can't imagine why anyone, including Troy, would spend a fortune on Indian and colonial relics. The desert practically begs for modern designs," Townsend said. "But then Troy is mad. Always has been. If it weren't for his wife, I wouldn't be here." There was a twinkle in his gaze just before he nodded toward where Troy and Bertoleo were standing. "Go ahead. Introduce yourself. Bertoleo is nondescript, but his master is a fascinating man. You won't be disappointed."

"Since I have no expectations, I'm sure I won't," Lara assured him.

Townsend smiled a secretive smile. "When you're ready for more plain talk, Lara, come and see me. I'll be here for the week. I'm staying in my home not far from the canyon. I'd love to chat."

Bemused, Lara studied him. Everything Rupert Townsend said and did had a purpose. The man was a major power player...like her father. She found it disconcerting to be Rupert's focus. So disconcerting, in fact, it made her feel like running away. Only sheer determination enabled her to stand her ground. A commotion at the door drew her attention.

Townsend clicked his tongue. "Well, really. What was Eliza thinking to invite them?"

Lara turned and saw a very unusual couple standing in the doorway. Black leather from head to toe. The man was very tall, with long, curly black hair. His leather vest had short sleeves, which showed off an incredibly detailed dragon tattoo. The woman's hair was just as dark...artificially dark, dyed to match her partner's. She appeared incredibly delicate and pale against the mass of black hair and clothing, and she had more piercings in her ears then Lara had ever seen on one person.

"Who are they?" she asked Rupert.

"Avery Johansson and his wife. They have a very large estate here in Sedona." He added, "He's the lead singer for some rock band, something about geckos or lizards or something."

"You mean Dragonsong?" Lara asked.

"Yes, that's it. Some trendy, silly name. He's apparently worth more than your father, but if you ask me, they have no place here."

Lara glanced sideways at Rupert. "We *are* here to earn money for the school, Mr. Townsend. If he's as wealthy as you say, then Eliza was right to invite them."

He made a rude sound. "Some things just aren't worth sacrificing."

Taking a breath to control her temper, Lara said, "I believe my mother's school is worth it. If you'll excuse me, I think I'll introduce myself." She crossed the room toward the couple and the small group gathering around them.

The woman's green gaze focused on Lara. Then she tugged at her husband's arm. Once, twice.

He interrupted his conversation with Troy. Seeing his wife's gaze locked on Lara, he nodded. "Yeah, Babe," he said as Lara walked up. "She must be the one."

"Excuse me?" Lara asked.

"My wife knows things," Johansson said with a nonchalant shrug. "She felt certain we would meet someone important tonight."

The woman remained silent, studying Lara.

"Well." Lara felt a little uncomfortable to be the center of everyone's attention.

Troy smiled, a teasing, tongue-in-cheek smile.

The couple's entourage looked at Lara like she might sprout wings and fly any minute.

"Well," she said again. Then she extended her hand to the woman. "I'm Lara Fallon."

"Milly Johansson." The woman sounded shy…very timid. A slight smile fluttered over her black lipstick-coated lips.

Lara took her hand, and a jolt of energy passed between them. Lara raised a surprised gaze to the young woman's face.

Milly's half-smile broadened. "Yes, you're the one," she said, just above a murmur.

Speechless, Lara stared at the unusual couple.

Milly glanced at her husband.

Without a word, he turned to Troy. "Show me

your house, man. I hear it's too cool."

They headed off and the entourage followed, leaving Lara and Milly standing in the foyer.

"I'm sorry we messed with your mind." The young woman's voice was barely more than a whisper.

"Don't worry. You're not the first to do that tonight."

Milly nodded. "I thought there'd be turmoil."

"You thought?"

The woman shrugged. "I get feelings, know things I shouldn't know."

"You mean you're psychic?"

"No. Jesus is a close personal friend, and I talk to Him a lot."

The sincerity in the woman's tone stopped her from laughing. "Lots of people say the words, but I believe He really is your friend."

"You have no idea where I'd be now if He had not come into my life."

"I think I can imagine."

Milly smiled, a sweet shy smile. "Yes, I suppose you can. I was pretty sure I'd meet someone important tonight, and then, we'd know what to do about the school."

"The school?"

"Avery and I have been praying for weeks now about becoming donors. We haven't had a lot of answers, but there was a lot about a person who would be important to us."

Shifting slightly, Lara said, "And what did you learn about that person?"

"The Lord put it on my heart to pray for you because you were headed for great danger."

A tingling started in the pit of Lara's stomach but

she smiled. "A palm reader told me the same thing when I was twelve. She also said I would meet someone tall, dark, and handsome who would change my life."

"It's OK." Milly's reply came quickly. "You don't have to believe. Most people don't at first. It's only important that we believe and pray, and we have been. But it hasn't made our decision any easier. We won't make a move until it's resolved."

"What's resolved? I don't understand."

"Danger comes in a lot of forms, Lara. It doesn't always mean physical danger. It could mean a crossroads, a decision. I think you'll have a decision to make and it could mean success or failure."

Lara's smile faded. "Now, I know this is way out there, Milly, since I have nothing to do with running the school or its success."

"You will."

Shaking her head, Lara took a deep breath. This soft, faithful woman so close to her own age made her feel protective. Her normally rigid guard slipped a notch more. "So you won't make a commitment until I come to some grand decision. Did your prayers tell you how I'm supposed to commit to this decision?"

Milly frowned. "No. They're never explicit. I'm not a fortune-teller. The Lord just makes me aware so I can deliver His message. But it's always best to follow your heart, don't you think? God speaks to your heart and it usually leads you to the truest course."

Thinking of the afternoon she'd spent with Brett, Lara said, "I'm not sure, Milly. In fact, right now, I'm not sure about anything."

Milly nodded. "That's why you're headed for trouble. You have to find out what's in your heart,

Lara. If you want, we can pray right now."

Lara quickly shook her head and looked around. All she needed was her mother's friends watching her pray with this strange, fragile creature. "No, no...that won't be necessary."

"Yeah, you're right. You're not ready to listen. But I'll keep praying." Suddenly, she lifted her hand in a shy wave. "It was good to meet you, Lara Fallon." With a slight smile, she turned and followed her husband and his entourage.

Lara stood alone for a few silent moments, not certain if she should laugh or run for her life. Suddenly, she'd had enough. Turning, she headed for the French doors at the other end of the room. But she had to cross the room and that meant moving through the crowd. She couldn't take two steps without someone stopping her. There were smiles and kisses and appropriate responses, but what was in their eyes was more telling.

A middle-aged woman stopped her. "Lara, it's so good to see you." Those were her words, but her eyes said, *I didn't think you'd ever get over the accident and get on with your life!*

Her mother's favorite designer, a distinguished man with silver in his hair, purposely made his way toward her. "Darling, you look fabulous," he mouthed. But his look said, *Your dress is a rag. Sara would have dazzled us with a new creation. Simply dazzled us.*

One of her former schoolmates, Cynthia Halton said, "Brett must be delighted to finally have you here." She meant, *Next time you leave his side, I'll be there.*

What they didn't say beat at Lara like unseen blows. Milly Johansson's weird, blunt talk had been easier to take. Relieved to finally reach the balcony, she closed the doors behind her with a snap.

Plain talk. Rupert's words came back to her. What she wouldn't give for some plain talk or an honest encounter.

Like the one she'd had with Alex on the balcony?

Purposely, Lara shut him out of her mind. He was a professional with two faces and two names, Alex Summers, the man and Alejandro Summers, the performer. Whatever he called himself, he was a practiced charmer with a patroness to maintain him and a string of lovers around the world. He made it his business to find out what women wanted and to give it to them. There hadn't been any plain talk or honesty in their encounter.

Well, actually there had been something real. Her response to him had been pure lust, a response Lara was not used to dealing with. It had set her off balance and made her even more susceptible to Alex's smooth ways. The next time, she'd be more alert, more prepared. He wouldn't catch her off guard like that again.

Cold air slithered over her. Now that the sun had set, all warmth disappeared. The desert night felt wintry, cold, and empty. The sky was the night's only saving grace. With no lights to hamper them, the stars twinkled like brilliant diamonds.

Rubbing her arms, Lara gazed upwards, savoring the sight of black velvet studded with diamonds. The air was so crisp, so pure, and the stars seemed closer, as if she could reach out and touch them. They were more real to her than the people inside.

Her problem in a nutshell: Her father called her a dreamer, chasing after things that didn't exist, would never exist. The real world, her world, was in the rooms behind her, and she was having more trouble connecting with that than she was the stars.

The crowd had moved to another room. Obviously, it was time for Alejandro to play.

Lara wouldn't stay. The entertainment was bound to be as disappointing as everything else in this day. Maybe jetlag *had* colored everything with a dusty, desert haze. Tomorrow, after a good night's rest, everything would be as it should.

She walked down the balcony, past the room where she'd seen the guitar, and entered the house through the French doors she'd originally exited. Near the front entrance she stood poised, her hand above the long-handled doorknob. The first strains of guitar music echoed over the empty foyer, its pure tones halting her and capturing her attention.

Was it Alex—Alejandro, whatever he called himself, playing? Were those long fingers that had stroked her cheek now strumming the strings of the instrument? The chords of Flamenco music floated and flowed over the Spanish tiles and candelabra. Haunting and forlorn, they echoed through the halls, calling to her as if searching for something lost.

Suddenly, she wanted to see the guitar, the instrument that could make such sounds...and the man who could play it. Would its surface gleam like something alive? Would he elicit sounds from it the way he'd pulled emotions from her? She had to know. Lara followed the music to the great room where the lights had been lowered.

Alex sat on a stool before a large fireplace. Orange flames danced in the center of a half-moon-shaped white hearth, hiding the man in shadows. In his hands, the instrument glowed with golden light as his dark fingers leapt over the strings.

Fascinated, Lara slipped into the shadowy crevice of the archway and watched as he started another haunting Flamenco song—one reminiscent of passion and pain, of souls lost and found. When she closed her eyes, Alex's story came to her. Gypsies, black nights, and campfires. In her mind's eye, a dark-haired beauty danced and swayed through the crowd, mesmerizing everyone to the strains of the guitar. Lara envisioned Juan Miguel, love and passion written in his features, as his gaze followed Lucia around the campsite. The image was so clear, so vivid, Lara could almost feel the heat of the fire and the cool air at her back.

The cadence of Alex's palm striking the guitar pounded a beat in her heart. She wanted to move, to dance, to spin around and around, skirts flying, hair wrapping around her body, her soul spiraling up like the smoke from the fire, disappearing into the vast, star-studded sky. Faster and faster. The rhythm of the guitar matched the pulse of her heart and suddenly…it ended.

Lara opened her eyes.

Alex had pressed his palm to the guitar so that all pounding ceased.

But not Lara's heart, it throbbed. Her breathing sounded ragged. Her chest heaved, and she pressed a hand to it.

When she looked up again, Alex's gaze was fixed on her. Even though she stood hidden in the shadow, across a room full of people, he had found her. The crowd continued to clap with noisy appreciation, but Alex didn't even acknowledge them. His gaze held Lara's, and his dark eyes flashed as if caught in the light of a campfire.

Without looking down, he started another song. He plucked at the strings and a pure, bell-like tone filled the room. The guitar became a chorus of church bells, somber, slow, and pristine. Alex sang, his voice deep and sorrowful, matching the bell's sad sound.

Behind him, Bertoleo pounded a slow, rhythmic beat on the face of his guitar.

Alex's voice rose and fell, like a mournful plea.

Something inside Lara wanted to answer that plea, to ease his suffering. Alex's fingers danced across the strings. They moved with such fluid grace, they hardly seemed to move at all. And yet, each note echoed with distinctive cadence, touching her heart and soul.

Alex ended the song and dipped his head as the crowd applauded. He launched into a new one. Flamenco again, but this tune had a different beat, a faster pace. Alex's fingers flew over the strings, running up and down the chords. It was dance music, pure and simple.

Lara tapped her toes and swayed against her will. Closing her eyes, she leaned back, certain she'd never heard anything quite so compelling. Vibrant, but airy, pure joy...like golden sun spilling into a darkening valley. Like the sunset she'd just watched...shared with Alex.

Could it be? Her eyelids flew open. Was it her imagination? Alex was still watching her, waiting. He smiled, and she knew he'd seen recognition in her features. He let his fingers run down the strings in one triumphant chord. Then he slapped his hand against them to hold them perfectly still.

Silence filled the room once again.

After a moment, startled applause pierced the

quiet. The people on the couch rose to their feet, clapping.

Alex nodded, but never spoke. He was intent, already focused on the next piece. He and Bertoleo worked without words, Bertoleo anticipating Alex's next song. They performed as if no one else was in the room...until Alex looked at Lara and a sense enveloped her as if she were a part of something rare, something imbued with antiquity and the passion of the ages.

With each new song, Alex was speaking to her, sharing an image or an emotion through his music. She envisioned running streams, horses galloping through fields and couples swaying together in soft embraces. No music had ever touched her the way his did. For forty-five minutes, she stood still, enthralled as she shared his visions. And when it was over, she couldn't clap or cheer. She was too full of wonderment.

He carefully placed La Guitarra in Bertoleo's hands.

People rose to their feet. Others followed, giving him a standing ovation.

Alex stepped forward, headed straight for Lara.

Her heart jumped into her throat.

The crowd surged toward him, blocking his way, but not before some realized his intentions. Heads turned in her direction.

Milly Johansson whispered something to her husband, and he smiled.

Lara imagined the questions forming in their minds, intrusive questions.

No matter who or what Alex's reputation was, his music was the most honest thing she'd ever shared with anyone. It was real. The thought terrified Lara.

She pushed away from the wall and fled far from Alex and the gaze that singled her out. In moments, she slipped into the night.

The moon had risen, dazzling and full, casting a silvery glow on the walkway as she came to the large, three-bedroom guesthouse she shared with Brett. By the time she closed the door, she was shivering from the cold and her wayward thoughts.

Wrapping her arms around herself, Lara leaned against the bedroom door and closed her eyes. Almost immediately, she heard his music. Haunting refrains. Mournful cries. Rhythmic beats. Clear and vivid, as if Alex and La Guitarra were in the room with her.

Furious, Lara stalked across the room. She punched the on button of an alarm clock/radio atop a bedside table, and the pulsating beat of rap music filled the air. Moonlight spilled into the room through her open shutters. The canyon spread out before her, easing into the valley below. Across from her window, the canyon wall climbed a short way before abruptly ending. Above it was the brilliant moon and the star-studded sky. She raised the blinds so there was nothing between her and the endless night.

It made her think of a gypsy fire. She needed to forget.

Spinning, she turned up the volume of the radio. She moved to the rap song, swung her hips and spun, letting the abrasive beat pound the sounds in her head into silence. Finally, she was tired and breathing hard. Slipping out of the blue dress, she fell into bed. Just as her eyes drifted shut, she remembered she'd left the party without a word to anyone.

3

Lara jerked upwards in bed.

Like something she'd absorbed into her skin, Alex's music had oozed into her dreams, bringing visions of campfires and him…watching her. His gaze caressed, like the touch of his long fingers. The sensations lingered even as she tried to slow her breathing and adjust to the bright daylight coming through her open blinds.

Sunlight poured into the room. Bright and full of reality, it should have dispelled the images. But it didn't. Leaning back on her elbows, she studied the canyon in front of her. Bristly pine trees were thick with sticky sap and pokey pinecones. Massive rocks, gritty with dirt and sharp angles. Bushes with shiny leaves. The stuff of reality. The real world.

The Alex in her dreams was a specter of the night, made of moonbeams and wishful thinking. The real Alex was very different. Too cultured. Too sure of himself with a string of lovers he knew how to please. He had probably used the guitar story on all of them…and she'd fallen for it.

No. She'd fallen for his music. It had captured her heart and made her want to dance. For her, dance was medicine.

When the doctors told her she might never walk again, she turned to dancing. Growing up, she'd taken a few classes and ballet had always been a part of her life.

In her mother's opinion, however, Lara's position as an heiress and a patroness excluded participation. She had a role to fill, a responsibility to foster all of the arts, not just one. And so, Lara had never been allowed to take more than a few basic ballet classes.

She didn't realize how much she wanted to dance until the ability to walk was taken from her. Then the desire grew until it became an obsession. After countless operations, pins and plates, her legs began to heal. Lara used her obsession to drive the healing process. Someday, she vowed she would dance.

Her father hired a tutor and day after day, she pushed herself, stretching unused muscles, demanding they conform to the rigorous ballet dictums. After a while, she'd been able to hobble about in a parody of dance, but recently she'd begun to move with grace.

She'd become very good at ballet, something she'd accomplished in hours of practice after Brett, Troy, and Eliza had moved away. Her accomplishment was one of the first things she'd wanted to share with them when they came together again, but it hadn't happened.

Lara hadn't heard Brett come in last night and now she wondered how she would explain her abrupt departure. Rising to her elbows, she saw a note under her door.

Lara,
I knew you were tired so I let you sleep in. I will send a car to bring you to the school at nine thirty.
Brett

She'd overslept. The school's dedication ceremony

was scheduled for ten a.m., and it was nine now. She barely had enough time to hop in the shower. Angry about Alex and his distracting music, she hurried to the bathroom.

Twenty minutes later, she slid into black knit pants, chose a silky turquoise top and zipped a short, black jacket over it. She waited by the front door for the car to arrive.

Attired in his usual black suit and sunglasses, the security man nodded and held the door for her. Lara stepped in and settled back.

They traveled down the two-lane road to the canyon floor. The pine trees disappeared, giving way to desert brush and finally, the small resort community of Sedona.

The town's architecture was a curious mixture of leftover fifties and modern buildings. Like a town that had grown too fast, truck stop cafes were interspersed with strip malls. Boutiques stood next to insurance offices and everywhere, the incredible rocks dominated everything. The only skyscrapers were the massive red bluffs of the canyon walls. Even the fast food chains paid homage to them with their rusty colors and Southwest décors.

The car passed through town. Nestled far off the main road, Lara saw the Fallon School of Art. The huge three-story edifice had the sharp angles and corners of modernistic design. A black cloth covered something on the large flat face of the gray-colored building.

The school's parking lot was full of cars, so the driver took a small delivery road around the scrub pinions to a side lot. He parked, and then led Lara through a maze of walkways to a raised dais in the front. Seeing Brett, Lara hurried forward.

She and Brett had discussed the agenda many times. She played an important role in the opening ceremonies, but thanks to Alex, she'd managed to forget about it. Now she hurried up the steps, regretting her hurried arrival. She should have been here, should have prepared.

Brett took her hand and gave her a smile that never quite reached his eyes. Turning, he gestured to Troy. "Any time you're ready, I think we can begin," he said.

Troy rose from his seat beside Eliza and walked to the microphone. "Ladies and gentlemen, if I could have your attention, please."

The crowd in front of the dais shifted and focused.

"As many of you know, this has been a long time coming," Troy continued. "Sara Fallon and I talked about a school like this when we were struggling students. Over the years, our paths took different courses, but we never forgot the dream of creating a school for children with special talents. It's taken two years of hard labor for Brett and I to bring the school to this point. We are very conscious that it would never have come this far if not for the generous support of Daniel Fallon and Sara's many, many friends. Because so many of you have been a part of this process, we've asked you to join us here in Sedona for a week of celebrations…and we'd like to start it off with a tour of the facility of which we're all so proud."

The crowd clapped. Troy raised his hands to quiet them. "But first, I'd like to spend a little time talking about the lady who was determined to see this school come to life. Brett…."

Releasing her hand, Brett stepped up to the microphone. He took a moment to adjust it to his height and all the while, Lara remembered what Rupert Townsend had said about her father.

Why *wasn't* he here? He should have been the one to recite her mother's humanitarian awards, the benefits she'd supported and the years she'd devoted to the arts before the car crash that killed her and almost paralyzed Lara.

As Brett spoke of the crash, the crowd turned to her, the daughter who looked so much like Sara Fallon, but was really just a pale imitation.

Lara hated this kind of attention, hated being compared to her brilliant, shining mother. No matter how hard she tried, she knew any comparison would find her lacking. She could almost hear the whispers.

How could Sara and Daniel Fallon be the parents of such a lackluster child? Surely, some of their glow had to wear off on her!

But no, there was no glow. Not even a shine...except maybe from her sweaty palms. She wanted to wipe them on her pants, but automatically heard her mother's voice reminding her she was a Fallon. Her father's representative. An example for everyone. Sweating somehow didn't seem appropriate.

She glanced at Brett again, hoping he would finish his speech, that the sight of him would instill her with confidence. But all she could see was his dark clothing. Black knit shirt with a high collar, jacket and pants.

Except for a small triangle of turquoise at her neck, she wore black, too. New York attire. Appropriate for any occasion. But here, against the colorful red rocks and deep blue skies of Sedona, Arizona, they seemed oddly out of place...like two big, black vultures poised on a perch.

Her gaze swept over the crowd and, suddenly,

there was Alex. He stood a few rows back. His loose, flowing shirt and dark pants had disappeared, giving way to a pair of blue jeans and a crisp, green and blue plaid shirt. He looked comfortable and far too casually dressed for such an affair. But somehow, with the red bluffs behind and the miles of desert surrounding them, his manner of dress seemed more appropriate then hers and Brett's. She glanced back at Brett.

He'd stopped talking and was staring at her expectantly.

Oh, no! She'd missed her cue. Or had she? She paused a moment more, hoping he would give her some sign.

He just stared, a slight frown creasing his forehead.

It was time.

Taking a deep breath, she turned and pulled the black cloth covering off the school logo on the wall. The silky cloth slithered in the silence and the large art splatter design appeared. The multiple colors glistened in the morning sun. The words Fallon School of Art flashed with gold, and everything shimmered with brightness and hope.

People clapped again.

Brett raised his hand and gestured to the building. "Ladies and gentlemen, please join us." Brett took Lara's arm, leading her down the platform steps.

The crowed surged forward. Her father's money had built the school but it took the influence of her mother's friends and associates in the art world to create the "buzz" necessary for its success. The school had been the talk of the art world for two years. Everyone—including Lara—was anxious to see what Sara's dream and Daniel's money had wrought. Lara's anticipation built.

Inside, the building was cool and well lit. One entire wall of glass looked out upon the open desert. Bookshelves covered the other side of the room and the smell of new bindings filled the air. A massive gray and brown flagstone fireplace straddled a corner, dominating the room. Arranged beneath it in a semi-circle, brown leather couches and cushions invited long reading sessions or periods of relaxation and visitation.

Heading for the fireplace, Brett stepped onto the stone hearth.

"This is the grand meeting room," he said, addressing the crowd. "We'll welcome newcomers here, hold lectures and special meetings. We see this as the heart of the school, a place for inspiration and companionship. We'd like to share the other two important sections with you, the classrooms and workrooms. I'll lead the first group and Troy will follow with another."

Stepping down, he took Lara's arm.

A small group formed around him, Milly and her husband among them. She nodded to Lara and ducked her head.

When about half the crowd had formed, Brett headed down the hall. He led them through the bright classrooms designed for maximum light and beauty. Most had large windows that looked across the desert. One spacious art room faced the back of the school and a majestic red bluff approximately one hundred yards away. The rock's ragged, sharp face seemed to have been sheered off, a direct contrast to most of the gentle bluffs surrounding Sedona. This arresting rocky crag was different.

Lara stepped closer to study it. Striations created

different shades of red and gave the rock texture. Stunted pine trees poked out from nooks and crannies. Beautiful. It pleased her to think of the school's students surrounded by such wonders. She turned to say as much to Brett, but he was gone. The tour had moved on.

Startled, she was alone in the room...with Alex. She hadn't even seen him in the group! How could he make himself appear and disappear as if by magic?

He crossed his arms against his chest and studied the crag with rapt attention, as if looking for something. Without turning toward her he said, "Impressive, isn't it?"

She'd had dreams about this man and fallen in love with the music that flowed from his fingertips. That alone was enough to fluster her, but now, facing him, she was struck again by his vital presence. He dominated everything around him.

Lara was disjointed, unattached...as if she were still dreaming. "Yes. Yes, it is."

"What were you thinking when you looked at it?"

She couldn't remember. All she could think about were the long, lean fingers gripping the sleeves of his shirt. "I—I was thinking how wonderful this will be for the students."

"I thought so." His knowing tone jolted her.

"How could you know that? You don't know me and what you've heard is probably wrong."

He smiled. "I know you're a dancer."

Startled, Lara paused. "Who told you? Who have you been talking to?"

"No one. Everyone. You're often a topic of conversation here at your mother's dedication ceremonies."

Irritated, Lara turned toward the crag. "This was my mother's project. Why can't they talk about her?"

"Because you are a beautiful, silent enigma. You don't fit in. You choose sunsets over scintillating gossip, and spectacular mountains over tours where people are vying to be the first in line. They don't understand you."

Something in his tone made Lara turn. "And you do?"

That frustratingly knowing smile tugged at the corner of his mouth again. "I've already told you what I know about you."

She looked away. "If you've been listening to the talk, then you'll know you're wrong."

"I'm not. They are," he said with confidence. "If any of them took the time to really look at you, they'd see what I see, a woman compelled to touch an object of passion and love. Someone who can't stop herself from dancing when she hears Flamenco. You're a woman on the verge of discovering yourself, Lara."

His perceptive words unsettled her. "If you know so much about me, you also know I'm...promised," she said abruptly.

Instead of being put off, he smiled. "Ah, but Lara, there are...attachments...and then there are love affairs."

Lara bristled. "What's that supposed to mean?"

He shrugged. "You're here and Fraser's there. You don't strike me as a couple in love. If he's even looked at you, he has to see what's happening. He's a fool to leave you alone. I would never allow someone else to share this awakening."

Awakening. The word vibrated through Lara's body. It's what she'd experienced when she'd looked

45

at the sunset. As if she'd been in a long, long sleep and just opened her eyes. He had chosen the exact word to describe her feelings. Suddenly, she wanted to ask him more, to see herself through his eyes and maybe to understand. But a noise down the hall reminded her the tour had continued. Others would surely have noted her absence—hers and Alex's. Startled and flustered, she hurried out of the room.

Alex followed her, and they rejoined the tour.

Brett appeared to be the only one to have noticed them missing. As they eased into the crowd, he stumbled over his words and stopped mid-sentence. It was a moment before he started again. "We've provided as many comforts as possible," he said. "Many of our students will be far from home. We want their atmosphere to be as welcoming and conducive to creativity as possible. You've seen the classrooms and the gathering area, now I'd like to show you the workrooms."

"Where will the dormitories be?"

The question came out of the crowd, but Lara recognized Alex's deep, unmistakable voice.

"Excuse me?" Brett hesitated.

"I asked if we would be touring the dormitories."

"There are no dormitories."

Alex folded his arms. "Forgive me. You said the school would accept many younger students, those in the first, developing stages of their endeavors."

"Correct."

"So they will come from far away. They and their families will live here in Sedona during the course of their studies, and they will be expected to provide their own accommodations."

"Yes, that is the expectation."

Alex nodded. "I see. Then it is also to be expected your students will not be the most talented and promising of youthful artists."

Brett's features tightened. "What do you mean?"

Alex gave a shrug of his shoulders. "Students must first provide a very substantial tuition to attend the school. Then they must provide for their own food, clothing, living expenses. Your students will need to be among the very wealthy to attend the Fallon School of Art, Mr. Fraser."

After a small, stilted pause, Brett said, "We hope many of our students will find sponsors."

A wry smile twisted Alex's lips. "It's very difficult to find a patron at such a young age. Most sponsors prefer to wait until the artist gains consistency and a certain maturity."

"You're speaking from experience."

Brett was referring to Alex's patroness, the Comtessa de la Guerra.

Other people knew the story as well and heads turned sharply.

Lara heard the intake of breath as the group waited for Alex's reaction.

"If you wish to think so, Mr. Fraser, that's certainly your choice."

Anger flashed between the two men.

Lara and the crowd were silenced by the brewing storm.

Then Brett remembered where he was. Turning from a confrontation, he led the way down the hall. "If you'll follow me, I'll show you the rest of the workrooms. We're very proud of this portion of the school." He sounded stilted and uncomfortable as he walked them through workrooms designed to accommodate metal workers, sculptors, painters, and potters. Blow torches, pottery wheels. State-of-the art equipment. Everywhere Lara looked, she saw money, vast amounts of money.

She should have been inspired.

It had all been bought with the best of intentions. But after Alex's comment, it seemed ostentatious. An air of discord had shadowed the tour and no one was more aware of it than Brett. He stumbled over his carefully prepared speech.

At last, they came to a hallway that led to the administrative offices.

Brett paused, and then launched into a tutorial on the curriculum Troy and Lara's mother had developed years ago. He seemed on comfortable footing at last.

Lara relaxed and turned to see how Brett's adversary was handling his return to control.

Alex stood with his arms folded, a frown creasing his brow. His brooding look deepened and even before he spoke, Lara understood he meant to challenge Brett again.

"Mr. Fraser," he said. "Did I hear you correctly? Students will be subjected to four hours daily of standard academic studies?"

Brett's jaw tightened but he managed to maintain control. "Yes. Our students will need to continue their formal education."

"Without a doubt. But recent studies suggest some artistically gifted youngsters tend to be poor students. Their classroom performance usually does not match their intelligence...which indicates, Mr. Fraser, they learn differently. Their minds operate in unusual ways, which often accounts for their incredible artistic abilities. Given this information, I would think placing them in a standard classroom environment would not be conducive to a successful learning atmosphere."

Lara was surprised. These observances were not born from pleasing charm and banter. They had substance and depth. There was more to Alex than she'd first believed.

"They need to pass all the standardized tests," Brett replied, his tone short, terse.

"But they need not receive their information in the usual manner. To create this specialized environment for their artistic endeavors, and then to subject them to a method of teaching hundreds of years old seems fruitless to me. Frankly, I expected more."

"I wasn't aware you knew so much about education. Nor did I expect you'd take such a proprietary interest in the activities of the school. Are you intending to invest, Mr. Summers?"

Lara groaned inwardly. Brett was baiting Alex. Such behavior was so out of character for him, she didn't know what to think. At the same time, she couldn't help anticipating Alex's response.

He shrugged. "I am an educator, Mr. Fraser, a professor of history and music and, as you mentioned, a youthful musician. I was hoping to find a more relevant curriculum. Painting based on chemistry. Sculpting from mathematics. It would seem the most logical approach with these students."

Brett cleared his throat. "I'm sorry we've disappointed you, Mr. Summers, but with every new venture there are starts and stops. We're no exception, especially since we lost the genius and driving force behind our school." Brett cleared his throat again, and gestured to a connecting hall. "If you'll continue down this hall you'll find a door leading to the grounds where you'll discover unusual rock formations, picnic tables and a champagne brunch, compliments of Mr. Daniel Fallon. Thank you all for joining us here on this special day."

The crowd murmured its pleasure and dispersed.

Lara caught Brett's gaze over the crowd. When the last straggler had disappeared down the hall, Lara and Brett stood across from each other.

He ran a hand through his hair in a short abrupt movement. "Well," he said after the door had closed behind the crowd. "I couldn't have screwed that up better if I'd planned it."

Lara took a deep breath. "Brett, I've never seen you like this. Please, tell me what's going on."

A false, half-hearted smile brushed over his features. "I'm just stressed. Don't worry. Everything will be all right in a few days."

"Stop it," she said in a low, tight tone. "It's obvious something is wrong. If you expect me not to notice, then you must think I'm a child."

Raw honesty filled his expression as he met her gaze. "I think that's the point, Lara. The woman I know is hardly more than a child."

Something heavy dropped into the pit of her stomach. "What are you talking about?"

Brett gave a shrug of his shoulders. "I don't know you anymore, Lara. When I left, you were still recovering from years of trauma. There was vulnerability about you, a softness. When you stepped off the plane yesterday and walked toward me, it was as if I was looking at a different person."

"I'm healthier, if that's what you mean."

"That's not all, and you know it, Lara. I could read it in your emails and hear it in our phone conversations...you're not the person I left in New York."

"And...you don't like the person I've become?"

"I don't know how to take you. You're...different."

"Well, you're not the man who left New York. The Brett I know would never have compromised a business prospect by allowing his emotions to rule him."

"Don't you think I know that? I'm well aware of the mistakes I'm making. And *this* conversation is a classic example of what I'm talking about. You would never have spoken to me like this before."

"It's the truth. Are you upset because you don't want to hear the truth?"

"I'm upset because I'm not used to hearing it from you."

"That doesn't make any sense, Brett."

He ran a hand through his hair again. "I told you, I'm making lots of mistakes. Things are piling up on me and I'm not sure what to do."

"What kinds of things?"

He hesitated, as if preparing to tell her, and then shook his head. "This isn't the time or place to talk about it, Lara."

"When is the time? I've been here almost twenty-four hours and we've hardly even been together."

"I know, I know." He ruffled his hair for the third time. "I told you, things are piling up and I can't explain it all, but I want you to understand this is my problem, my fault. It's going to take me a while to sort it all out."

His words didn't comfort her. "Brett—"

A noise at the end of the hall interrupted her.

They turned to see Troy leading his tour in their direction.

With an apologetic smile, Brett kissed her cheek and headed toward the group.

Disappointed, Lara stalked toward the exit.

Outside, long tables had been set up on the gravel grounds and draped with white linen cloths. Crystal and silver sparkled. Large baskets of breads and pastries lured Lara forward. She moved blindly, smarting from her fight with Brett...smarting even more because it proved Alex right. Who did he think he was, intruding into her life in this way? And how dare he be so close to the truth?

She took a glass of orange juice and a small pastry and strode to the edge of the grounds. Her gaze roamed over the desert. The slight breeze was cool, but gentle. It brushed over her face, wafting the scent of pine and mesquite. She took a deep breath, and then let it out in a long, slow sigh.

The open space was a balm to her senses. The vast stretches of red-colored land, the endless blue skies soothed.

She'd traveled the world with her parents. By the age of ten, she'd visited every country in Europe and many parts of Asia. She'd spent her teen years in a Swiss finishing school, but nothing had impacted her as much as the last twenty-four hours.

The limitless sky made her feel as if she were soaring. If she just started walking, she would eventually step off the edge of the world and fly through the air like an eagle. Nothing would stop her. She would crest mountains, skim over stretches of endless land and see the distant cities. When she looked at the horizon, she felt invincible. She glanced back at the sparkling tables and the people milling about and wondered how they could stand there and not feel the same way, not feel the power racing through this incredible, majestic land.

But they stood in clusters, facing each other, and sipping champagne.

One other person faced the land. Across the grounds Alex stood, his arms folded, his gaze focused on the crag directly behind the school. His focus was so intent, so fierce, it made Lara wonder what he saw. She glanced at the mountain. Nothing was out of the ordinary.

She wanted to cross the space, to confront him, to find out what business he had interfering in her private life and why he'd attempted to sabotage their efforts with the school. She remembered how Milly Johansen had expressed doubts about the school and becoming a donor. Lara was certain everyone in the tour had come away doubting Brett and Troy's efforts, questioning their direction, focus and skills.

Why was Alex trying to destroy a worthy cause?

She wanted to have it out with him, but she didn't want to create a scene. The gossips already had enough to talk about. She looked toward the building, hoping to see Brett.

The last tour exited, made their way across the wooden deck and down the stairs.

She didn't see Brett or Troy.

Eliza chatted with a group of people, laughing, probably charming them out of more donations.

Lara didn't want to distract her so she stayed put.

Carlos Bertoleo broke away from a small group and walked toward her. Smiling, he extended his hand. "Miss Fallon? Mr. Townsend said I should introduce myself. He said you are great fan of Flamenco." Unlike Alex, Carlos had a heavy Spanish accent.

It took Lara a moment to adjust her hearing. When she did, she almost choked on her orange juice. She'd never given Flamenco music more than a passing notice until last night. What was Rupert Townsend trying to do?

"I enjoyed what I heard last night," she said after a moment's pause. "It was very distinct."

"I am glad. Much of what we played is traditional, but some is original. The last pieces were written by Alejandro and myself." Even Carlos called him Alejandro.

Why had he told her to call him Alex? The thought puzzled her until she realized she'd taken too long to reply. "Those were my favorites. Especially the last two. They were so…moving."

Carlos beamed. "I am delighted to hear it. I have a CD I will give to you."

Lara strove to maintain her polite mien. "I'd like that very much. How many CDs do you have?" she asked, trying to make conversation.

"Several. We would have more but Alejandro does not work year around. He has other pursuits." There was an edge in his voice. Was it bitterness? Or scorn? He turned away to study Alex across the grounds.

"You performed well together," she offered.

A small sound escaped him before he turned back to her. "I did well. Alejandro is a master." He said nothing more, and his gaze drifted back.

"Well, perhaps La Guitarra is the secret to his success." Lara attempted to lighten the atmosphere with the joking comment. It didn't work.

Carlos gave an abrupt shake of his head. "La

Guitarra is difficult to play. It does not hold a tone and the strings break over and over. But, still, he plays it like a master."

"Of course. It's magic." Lara tried to infuse laughter in her voice.

With a wry smile, Carlos lifted his hands. "The only magic, senorita, is in these. A player is limited by how fast they can move. Believe me, if there were magic in La Guitarra, I would steal it for myself."

This time, Lara could not mistake the yearning in his voice. She didn't understand Carlos, but his relationship with Alex intrigued her.

With another rueful smile, he tucked his hands away and said, "It is time I returned. We will play tonight, and I must practice. If you'll excuse me, I will see if Alejandro is ready to leave."

They said their good-byes.

Lara followed him, searching for an excuse. "Carlos, if he's not ready to leave, perhaps I can take you back."

He smiled. "Then I could give you the CDs. Are you sure it would not be an imposition?"

"No, I'm ready to leave."

"*Bueno*. Let us talk with Alejandro."

At the moment, there was nothing Lara wanted more in the world.

4

Carlos and Lara approached Alex.

His gaze settled on Lara, and her stomach jumped.

Carlos spoke to him in Spanish, and Alex replied.

Lara didn't understand the words, but Carlos was obviously displeased.

Alex gave an abrupt shrug of his shoulders and spoke in English. "Very well, if you wish. But if you insist on leaving now, take the car. I'll ride back with Ms. Fallon."

Carlos hesitated, waiting to see if Lara would object. When she didn't, he mumbled his good-bye and left.

"He seems upset," Lara said as he disappeared around the corner. "What did you say to him?"

"I suggested that he had practiced enough, but he insisted on returning to rehearse."

Lara shook her head. "Do you always say the unexpected? I've always heard practice makes the musician."

"Music is a reflection of life. If you have no life, you have no music."

"That sounds like something Juan Miguel would say."

He smiled. "You listened to my music last night? What do you think?"

She took a slow, deep breath. "I think I heard a sunset, if that's even possible, and a stream bubbling through the middle of Eliza's house. It was beautiful."

"It was life. Carlos believes music will give him life when it's life that will give him music. Since he doesn't allow himself to live, he'll never achieve the recognition he covets."

"Covet is a strong word."

He turned to face her, fixing her with his dark gaze. "I don't have time for weak words."

His intense stare made Lara uncomfortable. She tried to divert his attention. "Speaking of words, why don't you have an accent?"

"Dual citizenship. I was born in New York to an American father and a Spanish mother. When my parents separated, I returned to Spain with my mother, but I still have a home in New York."

"I see." Lara finally found the courage to meet his gaze. "Everyone calls you Alejandro. Why did you ask me to call you Alex?"

He smiled a slow, enigmatic smile. "Alexander Summers is my birth name. When I began to perform, it seemed inappropriate for Flamenco so I took my mother's version of my name as a stage name."

"That explains how you've managed to disappear from the public eye. You have another life and a name to go with it."

"It seems they are gossiping about me as well. Who told you I disappear from public life?"

Lara shrugged. "Does it matter?"

"Not to me. It suits me not to meet other people's expectations. I prefer the intrigue."

"Is that why you asked me to call you Alex? To intrigue me?"

"I wanted to do away with intrigue. I wanted you to know who I am, not the image I've created."

He made Lara's heart pound. "If you wanted to impress me, the image would have worked very well," she said in a low voice.

"If I wanted to impress you, I would have left the image intact. I want nothing false between us, just the reality of who we are."

Lara found it hard to breathe. "We don't even know each other. How can you talk about reality?"

"I know you, Lara. That's what makes you afraid. I know you better than you know yourself."

Once again his words rang true, but she wasn't about to let him know. "But I know nothing about you. Like, for instance, why you're so determined to see the Fallon School of Art fail?"

He turned from his intense study of her to focus on the mountain. "If the school fails, it will be due to the judgment errors of its creators."

"*If* the school fails? You all but signed its death warrant with your speech a few minutes ago."

"Do you honestly think I was the only one who noticed the problems? Those people were members of international corporations looking to invest their company dollars. They're renowned educators seeking worthwhile projects for their grants. Do you honestly think they didn't see what I saw?"

Lara could not bring herself to answer him.

He was so close to the truth it was humiliating.

"All I did was point to the obvious," he said. "It's now in the open so your friends can take action and correct the situation before it's too late. If they choose to stick their heads in the sand and pretend nothing's wrong then the school's failure is their problem."

"So you're saying you did us a favor by publicly denouncing our mistakes?"

"Actually, I did *them* a favor. I wasn't aware you had much to do with the school."

True once again. She hated how he always managed to hit the issue straight on the head.

"It bears my mother's name and is an offshoot of Fallon Enterprises."

One eyebrow rose in a speculative manner. "You sound as if I should be afraid."

"Warned, perhaps." At long last, she'd gained some semblance of control. "My father doesn't fail."

One corner of his lips quirked in a wry smile. "Then you have nothing to worry about, do you?"

Just like that, the conversation was over. His silence told Lara things she didn't want to hear.

Her father wasn't here, hadn't planned to be here. He had handed the project to Brett and Troy and washed his hands of the whole affair. It wouldn't be his failure.

Suddenly, she understood Rupert Townsend's comments of the night before. Rupert understood her father's motives. Brett probably did, too, and it must be the cause of his stress.

Everyone understood but Lara. She felt young and foolish, and all because of Alex. His uncanny ability to uncover the truth irritated her. She wanted to lash out. To tell him off, or to tell him to mind his own business.

But he'd turned to his study of the mountain. His dismissal was humiliating.

"What are you looking for?" Irritation edged her tone.

"What were you searching for when you viewed the desert?"

His turnaround surprised her. It meant he'd been watching her as closely as she'd watched him. That knowledge washed away some of the edginess, made her feel warm. Alive. Tingly. Lara licked her lips. He understood so much. If she told him what she'd been seeking, would he think her silly or romantic or would he say she was passionate?

Brett and her father would say she was childish or silly.

But what would Alex say?

Lara decided to take a chance. "I love the open stretches of the desert. They make me feel like I can walk forever and when I reach the end of the world, I can step off and fly. I think I'm addicted to the feeling."

"You like the thrill of flying?"

"No," she said with a slow shake of her head. "I like the feeling of freedom."

"Is that why you didn't approach me when you first came outside? Because you don't feel free to act on your own?"

"I'm not free. Like you said, everyone is watching me. Everything I do is fodder for gossip."

"Lara, Lara." He gave a sad shake of his head. "Gossip is a game weak minds play. A woman like you should have no time for weakness."

"Easy for you to say. You're not Sara Fallon's daughter." She perused the crowd. "When they look at me, they see her. They expect me to be like her, to talk and think like her."

"All the more reason not to give them what they expect."

Brittle laughter slipped through her lips. "Even if I didn't resemble my mother I'd still be Daniel Fallon's daughter. He's an empire builder and I'm his heir apparent, the weak link to a fortune. Any signs of frailty on my part and the vultures are on me."

"Is that why Daddy assigned his CEO to become his daughter's…intended? To protect her?"

His words pierced Lara like a spear of white light. Blinding clarity filled her being as she digested what he'd said.

Had her father "assigned" Brett to become her friend? After the accident she'd been emotionally drained and weak…vulnerable. Brett's word. He'd called her hardly more than a child. Easy prey for the men looking to get to her money. Had her father sent Brett to win her affections, to protect her? Was that the real problem with them? Now that she had healed, there was no need for Brett to take care of her. The realization made her feel manipulated and angry with the man who'd planted the idea. She turned on Alex.

"That's not how it is," she snapped. "In spite of what you think, Brett's my friend. Since the accident, he's been my only friend. If it wasn't for him…"

His fingers gripped her chin and lifted it. "There's no need to defend him. He's not my concern," he said in a low voice. "I only want you to know you don't have to fly to be free. You can do as you please."

"You don't understand what it's like."

"But I do. When I was seventeen, my father invited me to return to the States to learn his business. I was desperate for his attention so I took his suggestion. He didn't understand anything about my music or what I wanted from life. We fought constantly. Then one day, I woke up, booked a flight back to Spain and took off. It was the last time I spoke to him."

"You haven't talked to him since?"

"There's no need. Nothing has changed. I am not the man he wants me to be."

Once again, his words hit close to home. She

didn't meet her father's expectations. He needed someone stronger, someone with business savvy who could wield the whip of power in his mammoth empire and keep things on track. She wasn't that kind of person so he'd turned to young men like Brett, men who fit his mold.

"What did he want you to be?" Lara managed the question, but her voice didn't work quite right. She couldn't seem to find any volume.

"A businessman with a suit and tie. Someone like Fraser, chained by responsibilities and predictable."

She had a sudden vision of her father meeting Alex. They would clash at first sight. She could almost see the expression on her father's face and could well imagine the disdain on Alex's.

"You would never agree to be predictable," she said.

He trailed his fingers along her chin. "You see. You've known me less time than my father and already you understand me."

His whispered words made Lara tingle again. "But surely you don't always do what you please?"

"Right now I want to kiss you." His gaze fixed on her lips. "But I won't because you'll wonder about who's watching and what they're thinking. When I kiss you, I want you to think only of me."

Lara caught her breath. It was hard to remember anything but his touch, the surprisingly gentle grip from such strong fingers. "Surely, you aren't always immune to what people say about you? You must feel something when they gossip."

"I suppose I have my father to thank. Other people's opinions no longer have the power to hurt me."

Her father's opinion mattered more than all the others to Lara. She couldn't imagine a life without his forceful presence. "I love my father, and he loves me," she whispered.

Alex shrugged and turned to study the mountain in silence. After a long pause he said, "You asked what I was looking for. Rock climbing is a hobby. If I can find a path to the top, I'll climb it."

"Right now? Without the proper clothing or equipment? With everyone watching?"

He turned and met her gaze. "You yearn to fly, Lara, because you let everyone's expectations tie you down." With those words, he stepped over the small retaining wall and walked toward the mountain.

People turned as Alex's long stride cut the distance to the craggy mountain.

He was going to do it. In minutes, he stood at the base. Before she could even draw a breath he began to scale it. He moved swiftly, his long legs stretching from boulder to boulder with assurance. Obviously, he'd found a path. He climbed quickly, as if he was walking across a flat stretch of land.

Lara was fascinated by his economy of effort. Because she had almost lost the ability to walk, his steady, smooth motions seemed like a ballet. She held her breath.

Alex found handholds and started his ascent. Without the benefit of ropes or even proper shoes, he climbed up the cliff, one step at a time.

A crowd gathered at the block retaining wall.

Troy and Brett stood beside her.

"He's going to do what I've been dreaming about since I first saw the bluff." Troy spoke quietly.

"But you've never climbed in your life," Lara said.

Troy turned to her with a wry, tilted grin. "I suppose it's a guy thing. It looks like something that needs to be climbed. The challenge is too much to resist, even for an out-of-shape dreamer like me."

"Then what stopped you?" she asked.

His grin deepened. "Eliza needs me. She would never forgive me if I fell and broke my neck."

Pulse pounding, Lara turned back just in time to see Alex slip. His shoes slid, and he slipped down the mountain. Lara managed not to gasp but her heart pounded so loudly, surely Troy and Brett heard it.

Alex regained his footing and moved upward.

"If he falls and injures himself, he's going to owe you a lot of money for missed performances," Brett said.

"I don't care," Troy replied. "This is almost as entertaining as his music."

Brett shook his head. "It's stupid exhibitionism, and I don't have time for it." He stalked away.

Neither Troy nor Lara acknowledged his departure.

Alex had almost reached the top but a huge boulder blocked his path. Completely smooth, with no handholds, the sheer rock face protruded over the cliff with a straight drop off below.

"This is what I've been waiting to see," Troy murmured. "I don't know how he's going to get around the drop-off."

"Before he left, he said he'd only climb it if he found a path. He must have seen a way."

"Let's hope so, because frankly, I don't think he's the type to admit defeat and come down the way he went up."

Alex stretched. His fingers gripped the face of the

rock and disappeared as they dug into a crevice. His long, lean body extended over the rounded face of the boulder. Momentarily, his feet dangled as he hung suspended over the edge. Then he began to pull himself straight up.

Troy gave a low whistle.

Lara caught her breath.

Alex continued to lift himself almost three feet up the face of the rock where he found purchase for one foot. Using the strength of his leg, he pushed himself up the rest of the way. In moments, he was standing on top of the boulder, looking out over the desert.

The people began to clap.

Lara didn't think Alex could hear them.

Suddenly, he turned and disappeared.

"Where did he go?" she asked.

"There's a fire break trail on the back side of the cliff. The other side is a gentle slope. He's probably coming down that way." Troy was wearing a pleased, silly grin on his face.

"You like him, don't you?" Lara asked.

He slid his hands in his pockets. "I admire him. When I look at him, I see everything I could have been if I'd had the courage."

Surprised, Lara stared at Troy.

"Don't look at me like that," he said with a laugh. "I wouldn't trade Eliza or Christy for ten bachelor lifetimes like his. I just meant if I'd been stronger, I would be in a better place now. I've made many compromises. Too many."

"What do you mean?"

His gaze shot to the school. A troubled look passed over his features.

Lara gazed at the huge building. It was her

mother's dream and her father's ambition, but two of the men she cared most about were paying the price for it. Was it worth it?

Troy turned away from the massive edifice. "Ah well, I didn't compromise on my house."

The sadness in his voice tugged at Lara's heart. She gripped his hand. "And you do have Eliza and Christy."

The same silly, boyish smile brushed over his features. "Yes, I do, and I'll do anything to keep them safe and happy." Bending, he brushed a kiss across her cheek. "It's good to have you here, Lara. We've all missed your gentle soul. It's just what we need right now."

Stunned, Lara watched him walk toward the school. Gentle soul? Is that how they viewed her?

She didn't feel like a gentle soul. So much was trapped inside her, it wasn't possible to be gentle. She felt wild and unsettled, wanted to fight and argue and...to fly. Her gaze flew to the top of the boulder. She wanted to be up there with Alex, to feel the wind against her cheeks and to see the limitless desert in all its majestic beauty. But she was too afraid, and suddenly, she understood what Troy meant.

Alex was uncompromising. He'd lost nothing. The world and all its vitality was his for the taking.

Troy admired his courage and Lara found it compelling, like La Guitarra.

He had an exquisite, perfectly formed shape...uncompromising lines, glowing with vibrant life and compelling her to touch.

But touching Alex would be dangerous. Rupert Townsend said there'd been many women in Alex's life. He wasn't the staying kind, the kind Lara needed.

She wanted someone like Brett, a best friend, someone she could depend on, someone who would always be there. Becoming involved with Alex would be foolish and irresponsible when Brett was everything she really wanted.

Lara was so certain about her feelings, she almost said the words out loud. Catching herself, she looked at the people still milling about. Why was she waiting for Alex to return? The last thing she needed was to ride back into town with a man who made her shiver and could cast spells with his words. Turning, she took the path through the brush, looking for her car and driver. She would leave before Alex returned from the mountain and send the driver back for him.

She hurried through the mesquite, too rushed to enjoy the tart tang of sage and dry earth. But it was impossible for her to completely ignore it. The desert air seeped into her pores, bringing with it a wealth of new sensations. Coming out of the brush, Lara finally spotted the black sedan in which she'd arrived...and leaning up against its side, his long legs crossed at the ankles and his arms folded casually on his chest, was Alex. Lara stumbled and slowed her pace.

"You were in hurry. Do you have an appointment?"

He *knew* she'd intended to leave him.

"As a matter of fact, I do. I promised Eliza I would meet her at the house after the reception and I wanted to take care of a few things first. I was going to send the car back for you."

"There's no need. I'm here. It was an easy run down the back side."

Run? He'd just climbed a mountain and *ran* down it. He didn't look as if he'd even broken a sweat. And he knew her thoughts before she did. He overwhelmed her.

Suddenly, she was fighting a tide, a riptide sweeping the sand from beneath her. She struggled to regain her footing. "Troy mentioned something, but I wasn't sure. I didn't know whether to leave you or wait. Impulsiveness can cause problems for the people around you," she said in a tart tone.

Alex's chuckle was soft. "It must not have caused you too much trouble. You decided to leave without any hesitation."

"I said I was going to send the driver back for you." She sounded snippy. She was frustrated and losing control over…nothing. She couldn't even name the problem. But Alex knew and the more she struggled, the more he seemed to enjoy himself.

Taking a slow, calming breath, she looked around for the driver. Spotting him near the school entrance, she motioned. Lara reached for the door handle.

Alex's hand was already there. Their fingers collided. His warm, smooth touch reminded her that moments ago, he'd used those fingers to lift his body up the side of a mountain. The night before they'd run over the strings of the guitar with the skill of a magician. Those hands could do too much. More than one man should be able to do.

They intimidated Lara, and she pulled back her hand as if she'd been burned by fire.

Smiling, Alex opened the door and motioned her inside.

Lara hesitated. She would be trapped, forced to see his hands, to think about what they could do, to hear his voice and remember his songs. She didn't think she could bear it. She slid inside, feeling as if she was sinking into a warm pool of bubbling sensation. She scooted all the way across the seat.

When she was safe on the other side, Alex leaned into the car. "Since you have such a tight schedule, I'll find another ride. Goodbye, Miss Fallon." He shut the door.

5

Alex watched Lara's sedan until the dust settled. Then he brushed his hands across the thighs of his jeans and smiled. He'd been pursuing her so persistently, she hadn't expected him to leave her. The look on her face as he'd slammed the door was enough to carry him through the rest of the day.

Or was it? Would a small victory be enough to hold him or would he need more? He'd known the intriguing Miss Fallon just over twenty-four hours and she'd consumed his thoughts the entire time. That was unusual for him. So was the pursuit. He usually didn't chase women.

His problem was keeping them out of his life, creating space for privacy. When he did allow a woman into his world, she came freely, knowing full well there were no attachments, no promises. Two adults attracted to each other. So what was it about Lara that pushed him past his usual boundaries?

Her beauty was obvious...the kind of looks that made a man feel protective. She appeared too frail for the real world. And there were times when Lara really looked the part, like a lost little girl in need of a hug. But it was the other times that captured Alex's imagination—the moments when he caught a glimpse of what simmered beneath the surface, her zest for life, her passion for things simple and great.

She absorbed everything around her. She touched

it, tasted, and consumed it like a sun devouring meteors. Every time he saw her absorbing something new, he wondered if this would be the time the explosion would come.

Someone had told Alex the story of the accident. Lara had been preparing to graduate from her exclusive Swiss finishing school, and her mother arrived early to take her shopping for the event. A late cold snap created black ice and Lara's mother lost control of the car.

Lara spent the next two years in and out of surgery and recuperation. This accounted for her innocence, as if her development had been on hold while she struggled to survive. She had wisdom, the kind coming from loss and pain, mixed with naiveté. She didn't know herself or her capabilities. But now, healthy and strong, she was about to discover what she could do. Any minute, the awareness would come to her. Would it come as an explosion or a subtle shift? He loved watching her. The waiting fascinated him.

Or was his attraction based on something else? He glanced back at the Fallon School of Art. Was it because she and Fraser had an understanding? He'd met the man on two other occasions and they'd rubbed each other the wrong way on both. Fraser represented everything Alex disliked. Structure. Social acceptance. Power. His father would love Fraser.

Did Alex want Lara because she was a part of that? Not just a part, but the favored daughter. Was he attracted to her because she was the forbidden fruit?

He honestly didn't know. This trip had resurrected feelings about people and incidents from his life he'd believed long dead and buried. Being suddenly confronted by the ghosts of his past made him uncomfortable. His inner peace had been shattered...but his music had come alive. He'd played like he hadn't played for years and given time, he would write. He was inspired. Maybe there *was* something magical about Sedona.

He brushed his hands against his pants once more. Maybe he just needed to get his answers and get out of here. He glanced back at the imposing dark, glass-filled backside of the Fallon School of Art. A lot of money was tied up in the building...too much for its owner not to have taken an active interest in it.

Lara said her father never failed. Alex believed it. So why would he invest so much money into one project and then hand it over to two employees who seemed incapable of managing it?

The question piqued Alex's curiosity.

Daniel Fallon didn't seem concerned about the success of the school, so what was his real reason for building it? Could it be a cover for something else?

Those were UNESCO's suspicions. Fallon Enterprises was a multinational corporation dealing in international antiquities and estates, and sometimes served as a broker for museum pieces. The company had the resources and the means to finance and ship antiquities to any location in the world, and in fact did so on a daily basis. They'd had a squeaky clean record.

But recently, an unusually large supply of Chaco pottery had made its sudden appearance on the black market. An undiscovered cache, an ancient village or burial site, had been found and was systematically being looted.

Logical, wasn't it, to question the coincidental creation of the Fallon School of Art, very close to the source of this new cache of pottery?

Alex had served as an advisor to the international Convention on the Protection of Cultural Property. He was an ideal recruit...passionate about art and history, and always at the right place at the right time. In the past, his assistance had been advantageous to UNESCO and the work had been easy for him.

But this time, he suspected it would get tricky, especially if he didn't make another friend at Fallon Enterprises...one who wasn't quite so innocent and not forbidden. With a rueful shake of his head, he walked back to the building, looking for a way inside. The tour had given him the layout of the building...and Brett Fraser's office. That was a good place to start.

~*~

The drive through town was silent, empty. Lara told herself this was what she wanted, the best thing. Still, a few moments ago, life had seemed vital, more exciting.

When the car stopped at the guesthouse, Lara jumped out before the driver could help. Thanking him, she hurried to the front step. On the ground in front of the dark wood door was a Christmas bag with handles.

Lara shoved the tissue away to find three CDs inside. Carlos had already delivered his promised gift.

The tires crackled on the gravel as the car drove away.

Lara stepped into the sun to study the CDs.

On the first cover was a headshot of Alex. He leaned against the neck of the guitar, and couldn't have been more than twenty. His features were young, vibrant and crisp, his hair much longer. His long fingers wrapped around the guitar neck. A faraway, dreamy look in his eyes created a romantic pose and took advantage of his stunning looks.

On the next cover, he looked older with his hair tugged back into a ponytail. His position, his concentration, everything about him said he was actually playing the guitar when the photo was taken, as if his music was everything and the photo meant nothing.

The third CD was more recent. Carlos stood like a dim shadow in the background. Though his hair was shorter, a slightly smiling Alex appeared as he did now. His features had lost the youthful glow of perfection and appeared more mature, even a bit weathered…but still, his expression conveyed the idea he knew something no one else did.

Lara was beginning to believe he did. He possessed the secret of living, the key to a rich and fulfilling life. That was his mystique. The thing Lara found so utterly irresistible…as did every other woman he met.

He was too compelling, too attractive, and if she weren't careful, she would be another notch on his belt.

~*~

Lara arrived at the main house with ballet shoes in hand, only to find that Eliza had not yet returned from the reception. Fortunately, she had left instructions. The maid led Lara up the curving stairs and down the hall. Inside the room, she found ceiling-to-floor windows, a wall full of mirrors and a dance bar.

"Mrs. Madrigal said to make yourself at home until she returns."

"I can't believe they built a dance room." Lara turned around, eyes wide.

The maid smiled. "She said you would be surprised."

"Shocked is a better word."

"Well, you enjoy yourself. I'll send Christy in when she finishes her studies." She closed the door behind her.

A table in one corner held a CD player. Next to the table, a guitar rested on a stand, an open case beside it. Lara dropped her bag on the floor and fingered the guitar's polished surface. Images of her dream returned and she turned to the windows, desperate to escape the persistent visions.

The view across the canyon spilled into the room through the wall of windows, creating the illusion of standing outside.

Not wasting another minute, she untied her multi-colored wrap-around skirt and began to stretch. She was full into her routine when Eliza breezed into the room.

Lara jumped up from her warm-up mat. "Eliza, this is incredible. I hope you didn't do all this for me."

Her friend gripped both her hands. "Yes and no. I only have a few minutes before Christy gets here so I have to make this short." She hesitated. "You know, I've been planning this for two months and now the time is here, I don't know where to begin."

Lara squeezed her hand. "Start anywhere," she said in a low voice, "and hurry. You're starting to scare me."

"The time to worry was two months ago when my marriage was failing."

"Oh, Eliza, now I am scared. Your marriage is one

of the few stable things in my life. Please don't tell me it's about to end."

"I think things will be better now, with your help. For the last two years, Troy's life has been wrapped around this school. It's consumed him. I found myself with more and more time to myself…which I devoted to Christy. And Christy, being a healthy young animal, has learned to take advantage of her poor mother."

"She's eleven. It's her job to make you crazy. I'm sure I was just as obnoxious at that age."

"You were an angel."

"You should have talked to my mother about it. I'm sure she had a different opinion."

"I did, frequently. But your mother wouldn't listen. She wouldn't settle for anything less than perfection from you."

"Eliza, I've never heard you talk about my mother this way."

"It's true, Lara. She and I went round and round. How can you have forgotten the rows we had?" Eliza paused to stare to one side. "Of course, she was always careful to make sure there were no dissenting voices around you. She was incredibly strict where you were concerned." Eliza shook her head, as if shaking off the memories. "But that's not important now. What I need to tell you is that I've gone the opposite way. I've indulged my daughter so much, it's actually impacting her health. Troy warned me, but I was resentful about his time away from home, and I wouldn't listen."

"You're a good mother, Eliza. Don't you dare doubt it."

"Perhaps. You know, I wanted a house full of children, but we had so many problems, we were lucky to get Christy. Then when she was diagnosed with rheumatoid arthritis and I realized I carried the gene, I was overwhelmed with guilt. I've been parenting with that guilt, Lara. I can't stand to see her in pain so I do everything for her. I'm always available to her and now she's paying for it."

"It can't be so bad. It's only been six months!"

Eliza smiled a weak smile. "I'm making it sound worse, but I'm just worn out from the battles with her. I needed you to come and give me a shot in the arm."

"Funny, that's what Troy said."

"You should believe him. He's a very clever man, you know."

"Oh really? Is that why you listened to him when he said you were spoiling Christy?"

"No," Eliza said with a wry grin. "I didn't listen, and that's the problem. She won't make herself get out of her wheelchair. She sits in it and doesn't move. It's the worst thing that can happen to a person with R.A. There's a saying…if you don't use it, you lose it. That's what's happening to Christy. She sits there, feeling sorry for herself. Her muscles are freezing up. And she won't listen to me anymore. Our days start and end with arguments."

Lara grasped her hands. "Eliza, how awful. I should have been here to help."

"Actually, Troy became my knight in shining armor. He saved us from ourselves."

"But you said Troy was too involved with the school."

"He was, but one day he walked in on one of Christy's temper tantrums. She was yelling at me and saying awful things. I was in tears. Troy used this booming tone he's never used before. He told her never to speak to me like that again, and if she didn't apologize that very instant, she would spend the rest of the day in her room with no television and no phone."

"Wow. Troy said that? I can't imagine it."

"I know. Christy didn't believe it either, so she launched into an ear-splitting argument. He snatched her up from the wheelchair, carried her upstairs and dumped her on her bed. Then he took her phone and television out of the room and told her if she needed to go to the bathroom she could get up and walk. Her dinner would be on a tray by the table, and if she wanted to eat, she could walk to that, too. Of course, I objected, insisting she needed to eat to keep her strength up, so Troy grabbed my hand, left instructions with Christy's nurse and practically dragged me out of the house."

"This can't be our Troy you're talking about!" Lara exclaimed.

Eliza giggled. "Isn't it wonderful? He was determined and forceful and so passionate. There's a path behind the guesthouse leading to the top of the canyon. We walked up and sat down and talked for hours. We even watched the sunset. Troy said he knew he was losing us—Christy and me—and he was desperate to get us back. He said he'd spent years of his life and sank all of our money into the house but he would walk away from it tomorrow if we could be a family again. It was the most romantic thing he's ever said to me, Lara."

"Sedona sunsets seem to do that to everyone," Lara murmured.

"Maybe, but I know a sunset saved my marriage. Troy had almost given up. He couldn't fight me, build a school, and create a house that's more like a work of art."

"You sound resentful about the house," Lara said.

"I'm working on my attitude. I always wanted a home with toys, dogs running through and muddy floors from a backyard pool. This place is more like a museum." She paused.

"But—" Lara prompted.

"I know, I know! It's incredible. Every line, every feature blends into the canyon as if it were a part of it. And when you step inside, it's as if you're walking into another time and place. It's a piece of art, Lara, and quite frankly, I didn't think Troy could pull it off. You know, before we left New York, my glass pieces were selling better than his work. I think he felt his career was on the downswing. This house has inspired him and renewed his creativity. How can I be mad about something that's brought the sparkle back to his eyes?"

"Troy says it's the only thing he hasn't compromised. He also says it nearly cost him everything. He's not sure it was worth it."

Tears glistened in Eliza's eyes. "It's my fault. I made him feel that way and now I'm going to do what I can to make amends."

"What can you do?"

"For starters, I can go back to work. I haven't worked for over a year. I could have been selling pieces and helping Troy with his dream. I should have been taking care of my child and supporting my husband. Which brings me to you."

"It's about time," Lara teased. "I was beginning to think there wasn't room in this story for me."

Eliza gripped Lara's hands. "I'm going back to work. Troy built a workshop complete with a furnace behind the house. The furnace has never even been fired up. It's going to be hard, spending hour after hour out there, mainly because Christy thinks I should be spending all my time with her, but I'm going to work. While I'm working, I'd like you to be dancing with Christy."

"Dancing! You said she's in a wheelchair."

"So were you two years ago. If you can do it, so can she. Since the day her father dumped her on her bed, she's been walking more and more. Now she uses the chair as an excuse, and besides, she adores you. There's nothing she'd love better than spending hours with you. Will you do it?"

Lara threw up her hands. "I don't know if it'll work, but you know I'll try."

Eliza hugged her. "Thanks. I knew I could count on you and if I can just sell two pieces, it will help."

"Two pieces, Eliza? Are things so bad?"

She nodded. "I think so. Troy won't admit it, but he's already making plans to sell some of the antiques he bought for the house. And I know your father is footing the bill for this week. Troy didn't have the money. And then he and Brett had a major fight over the expenses, especially the guitar and Alejandro. Brett didn't want to hire him, but Troy insisted. As far as I'm concerned, Troy was right. Alejandro made this event. He's created such a buzz, people are calling their friends. I've had three calls this morning from no-shows, asking if it's too late to come."

"And you think it's because of Alex...I mean Alejandro?"

"I can't think of any other reason. Can you?"

Lara shook her head, feeling uncomfortable. "Alejandro's a very charismatic personality."

"Charismatic nothing. He positively exudes passion and mystery. This crowd is terribly bored and looking for something new. He's the perfect antidote."

"Funny. Rupert Townsend said the same thing about me."

"Rupert Townsend took the time to talk to you?"

"We've become new best friends. I can't seem to avoid him."

Eliza frowned. "What could you be doing that's piqued his interest? And while we're at it, what do you know about Sedona sunsets? I haven't seen you and Brett together long enough to exchange glances, let alone share a sunset."

A blush crept over Lara's cheeks.

Fortunately, the door opened and Christy wheeled into the room at a dangerous pace.

Lara barely avoided getting her toes run over as the child came to a skidding halt and threw her arms around Lara's waist.

Christy was a younger version of her mother. Petite. Red, curly hair, and freckles. But where Eliza had learned to use her flamboyant coloring, Christy didn't quite know what to do with it. Her hair was pulled back in a tight, unattractive ponytail with fuzzy escapees breaking loose. Freckles spread across her pale skin like dirty spots. She was all braces, elbows, and knees.

Lara's heart melted as she recognized the awkward age.

"I wanted to wait up for you last night, but Mother made me go to bed," Christy said.

Lara hugged her, shuddering at the slender feel of her body. "Seems to me she made the right choice. You feel like you need all the rest you can get. Have you lost weight?"

"Mother's been talking to you, hasn't she?" The

way Christy said the word "mother" could have been a curse.

Hackles rose on Lara's neck. "Yes," she said in a clear, firm tone. "She has. And why shouldn't she? She's my dearest friend and your mother. She has every right to discuss her concerns with me. Besides, I love you, too. If you're not feeling well, I have a right to know."

Christy ducked her head, looking somewhat chastised.

Eliza used the moment to make her escape. "Well, I'll let you two talk. I'm going to get to work. If you need me, I'll be in my shop." Without another word, she hurried out of the room.

Surprised, Christy watched her go. "What's she doing in her shop?"

"She's going to work."

"You mean really work...on a project?"

Lara nodded.

Christy slumped in her chair. "So much for being worried about me. Now both of them will be too busy to care."

Stunned, Lara grasped her hand. "Christy, you know that's not true."

"It is! You don't know what it's been like since we moved."

Taken aback by her vehemence, Lara tried another approach. "A few minutes ago, it didn't sound like you wanted her around. You were rude, Christy."

"I can't help it. She's making me crazy. She frets over everything and makes things into a big deal."

"First you're mad because she won't be here to fret over you. Then you're mad because she does. I don't understand."

Christy slanted her an angry glance. "I thought you were my friend."

Lara dropped to her haunches in front of the wheelchair. "I am. But I don't recognize the person in front of me. The Christy I know would never be rude or unkind. Tell me what's going on."

"I hate it here! My only friends are a thousand miles away in New York. They're having fun and growing up without me. I never see anyone my age and the way I'm going, I never will. And I'm tired of always being in pain and being stuck in this wheelchair."

"Christy, I don't get it. It's warm and beautiful here in Sedona and there's so much space. With your love of horses, I was sure you'd be riding every day in your own backyard."

Christy slanted her another angry look. "Don't you get it? I can't ride anymore. It hurts. Everything hurts." Christy spun the wheels of the chair so it turned away from Lara. "I should have known you wouldn't understand. No one does."

Her angry outburst hung in the air for a long while before Lara could muster the words to speak. Then she said, in a very quiet voice, "Don't I? That chair looks very familiar."

Surprised, Christy looked up.

Lara walked around to the front of the chair and pointed to the arm where her own initials were etched in the metal. "I thought so. It's the chair my father bought me when I left the hospital. I loaned it to your mother when you were first diagnosed because it was designed for a smaller person. I didn't need it anymore so I sent it to you." Lara squatted in front of the sulky girl again. "For a long time, Christy, I didn't think I'd ever get out of bed. Now look at me."

The little girl turned her head away. "It's...it's different for you. You had hope, something to look forward to. The only thing I have to look forward to is more pain and getting so twisted up I'll look like an ogre."

Lara took her hand in a firm grip. "Perhaps. But there can be so much fun first. Horseback riding. Friends. High school and college. All you have to do is use those muscles."

For the first time, Christy turned to her. "But it hurts, Lara. You don't know how much it hurts."

Tears formed in Lara's eyes. "Yes, I do know, honey. I do. When I first started dancing I had to use a cane."

A short laugh escaped from Christy. "A ballet dancer with a cane? You must have looked pretty funny."

"So funny, I wouldn't let anyone else in the room while I was working."

Christy's eyes widened. "I remember. You always locked the door while you were practicing."

"I looked ridiculous. I fell a lot and most of the time my clothes were soaked with sweat because it was so hard and hurt so much. Sometimes, I couldn't tell if it was sweat in my eyes or tears. But it was worth it, Christy. You should see what I can do now." Something jumped inside Lara. "Wait...you *can* see what I do! I've been so excited to show someone, but everyone's been too busy to watch. You can be the first. Will you watch me?"

A tremulous smile edged at the corners of Christy's lips. "Sure," she said with a shrug of one shoulder.

Lara smiled. "Thanks. And wait till you see. I'm so proud of myself, Christy."

A full-fledged smile spread over Christy's features. Did she even know it had escaped?

Squeezing the girl's hand, Lara rose and slid one of Alex's CDs into the player. She skipped from song to song, trying to find the right one. She really wanted to dance to the driving Flamenco beat that reminded her of a sunset, but it was too fast for the stretch workout she had in mind. She found a slower paced song and closed her eyes, listening to the rhythm, mentally moving through her routine. This one would do.

"Can you give me hand?" she asked Christy. "I need some room to work so I want you to start the song for me."

"I don't think I can reach it from my chair."

Lara had never heard such a lame excuse, and she wasn't buying it. "Sure you can. Just lock the wheels and slide up."

Christy raised her eyebrows with a doubtful expression, but wheeled the chair over.

After a few minutes, Lara nodded.

Christy punched the button, and Alex's music filled the room.

Lara closed her eyes and felt the rhythm. Smooth chords and a soft, pulsating beat flowed over her skin like the wafting of a breeze. She raised her arm in a tall graceful arc above her head and looped the other at her waist. Slowly, she rose to her toes, making the movement with excruciating precision and holding it until her muscles screamed for release. Then she stepped forward, her legs angled, her arms extended, forming perfect graceful arcs.

The music flowed in and around Lara. It lifted her

to her toes and pulled her into another world. She envisioned a dark night and brilliant stars sparkling above. Lovers entwined beneath a silver moon, their caresses as soft as the night. And always the gentle touch of the music encouraged her forward.

She lost track of time. All she could feel was her body, swaying to the music, stretching beyond its limits. Her muscles were taut and trembling and still, she bent to the music.

On her toes, arms lifted, she extended her leg in a graceful circle all the way around her body. Slowly, smoothly, she curled it behind her and bent at the waist, arching forward. When she was perfectly poised on one foot, she rose to a point with strength and poise, never breaking her arched back or the smooth straight line of her legs and arms. When she couldn't stand it a minute more, the music ended.

Christy clapped enthusiastically and then, stronger, firmer hands joined hers.

Lara's eyes flew open, and she turned to see Alex standing in the doorway.

6

Alex pushed away from the doorway and walked toward her. His larger-than-life presence filled the room.

Lara resisted the urge to step back and managed to stand her ground as he approached.

"I heard my music and couldn't resist discovering the source," he said.

"That was your music?" Christy asked in surprise.

Alex paused and turned. "Yes. It was mine." He extended his hand. "I'm Alejandro Summers, and you are?"

Christy took his hand, but her voice dropped to an almost inaudible sound. "I'm Christy."

"I'm sorry," Lara said, smoothly stepping in to cover Christy's youthful shyness. "I didn't realize you two hadn't met. Alex...Alejandro, this is Christy Madrigal, Troy's and Eliza's daughter."

Alex dipped his head in greeting, and then dropped to his haunches, bringing himself to eye level with Christy. "So you liked my music?" he asked.

She gestured to the guitar by the CD player. "My dad bought it for me. Senor Bertoleo's been teaching me a little. It's really hard. But you make it sound easy. Your music's cool."

Alex's face lit with a blinding white smile.

Lara almost laughed when Christy's jaw dropped. Even pre-teen adolescents were susceptible to the man's charm.

"Cool is not a word people usually use to describe my work." Alex seemed oblivious to the devastation he was creating. "But I like it very much. Thank you, Miss Madrigal. And I've never had the privilege of watching my music put to a ballet. I must thank both of you ladies for an unusual encounter."

"She was beautiful, wasn't she?" Christy said, wistfully. "I wish I could do that."

Seizing her opportunity, Lara said, "You can. All you have to do is start working your muscles. I'll help you, Christy. Together we can get you up and moving."

Christy wouldn't raise her gaze to meet Lara's. She gave an abrupt shake of her head. "What's the point? By the time I learn how to do that, my hands will be twisted and I'll look like a nerd trying to be graceful."

Lara wilted.

Above Christy's head, Alex caught her eye.

"You haven't told her, have you?"

Lara's lips parted in puzzlement.

Not waiting for her reply, Alex dropped to his haunches once again. "Lara has learned something very important about dancing, Christy. I'm surprised she hasn't told you about it."

Christy looked up, first at Lara then at Alex. When he didn't continue, curiosity won out. "What?" she asked.

Alex flashed his stunning smile. "Lara has learned that it doesn't matter what other people think. The only thing that's important is how it makes her feel. She loves to dance, and so she does it. It doesn't matter if she looks bad because she doesn't care how other people see her."

"But she looks beautiful when she dances."

"That's because she stopped caring about how she looked and focused on how dancing makes her feel. Pretty soon, what was going on inside there," he pointed to Christy's heart, "started to show. Now she looks as beautiful on the outside as she is on the inside."

Christy hunched even lower in her chair. "You sound like one of those stupid after school kid's shows. 'Brush your teeth three times a day and nothing bad will ever happen to you.'"

Lara caught her breath at Christy's rude tone, but Alex started to laugh. "You know, the funny thing about those stupid kids' shows is that they repeat life's truths, Christy. Smart people pay attention."

Her gaze shot up. "You think I'm not smart?"

"I wouldn't waste my time talking to you if I didn't think you were clever enough to understand." His honesty was leveling, even for a rebellious pre-teen.

The child ducked her head, looking somewhat embarrassed.

"Maybe that's why I'm in this chair," she said in a very small voice. "What's inside me *is* showing and it's not very nice."

Tears burned Lara's eyes, but Alex never missed a beat.

"You're very unhappy, aren't you, Christy? What would change that...what would make you happy?"

She didn't hesitate. "Not being sick. I want to be a normal kid again."

Now the tears pooled in Lara's eyes and one slid down her cheek. She quickly wiped it away.

But Alex didn't succumb to Christy's self-pity. He

rose to his feet, shaking his head. "Why in the world would you want to be normal? I'd much rather be special. Unique. I'm happy to make music you call cool. I'd rather be someone like Lara who can hold a ballet pose until people want to clap and cheer. Why would you want to be normal when you could be unique?"

"I don't have anything special about me," Christy said, a frown wrinkling her brow.

"You have an illness that makes you unique even without trying," Alex said.

"Oh yeah, this is special," Christy snapped back. "I get to spend my day in a wheelchair. Whoopee!"

"It would be special, Christy, if you got out of it." Alex's voice was low and firm. "Not many people are strong enough to do that."

Christy's gaze jerked up. She stared at Alex, held his unwavering gaze a long while before the belligerent resentment melted out of her body. "It will hurt." She looked so tiny, and her voice reflected that shrunken size. "A lot."

"But the reward will be great. Did you see the look on Lara's face when she finished her dance? I did, and I won't ever forget it." Alex turned to Lara. His eyes portrayed pleasure and desire and so much more.

She had to force herself to turn back to Christy.

The child chewed at her lips, indecision written plainly on her face. But at last she spoke again. "Yeah, I'd like to feel like that."

"Then I'll make you a promise," Lara said. "If you'll work with me two hours every day, I'll take you riding."

Christy's gaze jumped up. "Do you really think I could do it?"

"I guarantee it," Lara said. "Even if it's only for half an hour. We'll find a stable and pick out a horse, and I'll ride with you. If I have to hold you on myself, you'll go riding."

The door opened, and Christy's nurse walked into the room. "I'm sorry to interrupt, but it's time for my patient to rest." She took hold of Christy's chair.

Lara placed a hand on the arm, holding it still. "Do we have a deal?"

Christy hesitated a moment. She glanced at Lara, and then back at Alex. "Do *you* think I could do it?"

His smile dazzled. "If I didn't think so, I wouldn't have wasted my time talking about it."

"You know what? I believe you." She caught her lip again, and then turned to Lara. "We have a deal."

Pleasure exploded inside Lara, and she grabbed Christy in a hug. "Great. I'll see you here precisely at nine a.m."

"I usually do my school work then."

The nurse spoke up. "I think we can work your studies around some time with Miss Fallon."

"Great," Lara said. "I'll be here at nine. Don't forget."

The nurse wheeled Christy out.

Lara turned around and found Alex's gaze on her. Suddenly, the room felt hot and far too small. She punched the button on the CD player. The music stopped. Lara pulled a towel from her bag. "Thank you for being so patient." She wiped her face, blotting the moisture from exertion. "Not many people would have put up with Christy's rudeness to get to the real heart of her."

Alex took the towel from her hand. Slowly, with his gaze fixed on his work, he stroked the cloth down the long length of her neck. "I could see you cared about her, and that made her someone worth my time." His murmured words sounded like a song...melodic, soothing, evoking a dangerous depth of emotion. He used his voice like an instrument.

It wrapped around Lara, filling her with joy.

"Besides, it's obvious she's a very unhappy little girl who needs a helping hand." He stroked the towel along her collarbone, leaving a vibrant tingle in its wake.

Lara struggled to suppress the ripples of sensation washing through her. "Is that what you do?" Even she could hear the breathless quality of her voice. "Find women in need and solve their problems for them?"

His eyes widened.

Bare inches apart, they locked gazes.

Flecks of gold and green flickered in the dark brown of his eyes, and suddenly, the tingling inside her turned to a slow burn.

"On the contrary." Alex dropped the towel and let his fingers flow over her skin like warm sunshine. "I find women who make me happy. Like you. Everything about you pleases me, especially when you danced. My music has never come to life as perfectly as it did with your beautiful body."

"My body is not beautiful, Alex. I have scars, plates and pins. They had to put me back together piece by piece."

"Broken glass lies sharp and jagged on the desert floor," he replied. "When the sun hits it, brilliant colors suddenly appear in the sky. Even though it's not whole, it makes something beautiful, more so because it comes from something broken." His fingers skimmed her lips with a light-as-a-feather touch, and he leaned in. He was going to kiss her.

She knew it…knew she had time to stop it. But she didn't.

"When you watched the sunset, your face held such innocence. I wanted to know who you were and what you were thinking. I still do," he murmured, and then he pressed his lips to hers.

They were warm, so warm they heated her numb body. Feeling surged through her, raw, primitive feelings. She wanted him, wanted to know his secrets, wanted to know what he could teach her and most of all, she wanted this wild, fierce joy to go on forever.

His fingers threaded through her hair. His other hand grasped her chin, framing her face as he kissed her eyes, her nose, her cheeks.

She moaned as delight swept through her entire body.

At the sound, Alex tucked her into the curve of his arm.

He made her feel beautiful, desirable, as if she were on the verge of a precipice, in danger of falling, and loving it still. She wanted to stay there forever but a warning bell sounded in the back of her mind. "No," she murmured. Placing her hands against Alex's chest, she shook her head. "No, I won't do this." She pushed free of his embrace and stepped back. "I won't do this."

Alex let his arms fall away. He rubbed his chin. "No, I suppose you won't." He folded his arms and stood, silent.

Lara's lips tingled. Her arms ached with emptiness and the answer stood just a few feet away. To keep herself from reaching for him again, she clenched her hands together. "Is that it?"

He shrugged and a half-smile flitted over his lips.

"Do you want me to force you?"

"No, of course not. It's just—the way you say it. As if you knew I wouldn't allow anything to happen."

"You would do what's expected. I know that much about you."

His words rankled her. "No. You expect I'll fall into line like the rest of your women. I won't."

"The rest of my women?" He shook his head and looked away. "Then why did you let me kiss you, Lara? Why did you let me hold you?"

She couldn't answer. She searched for words but none came.

"It's very simple," he said at last. "You let me kiss you because what you are feeling is real...and real love is magic."

She gripped her hands tighter, almost angry. "I don't need magic. I need a real marriage. My parents had that kind of relationship. They lived it every day of my life."

"Then why would you settle for something less?"

"I'm not settling."

"I've seen you with your intended, and there's nothing there. Maybe Fraser is a good friend, but that's it. Love should be magic, Lara. Anything less is second best."

"I'm not like you," she exclaimed. "I won't turn my back on Brett and everything he's done for me."

"Exactly what has he done for you? Maybe you should ask yourself what he received in exchange for his kindness. You are the boss's daughter."

Anger filled her. "You have no right to insult him just because you're looking for some action."

He stiffened, and his gaze grew hard. "I'm going to let that insult pass because I know you're confused and just a little afraid. Well, Lara, so am I." Grasping her arms, he pulled her close and kissed her again.

Fire raced through her veins. A tingling started deep inside and she weakened, felt the need for more. She was just warming up, reaching for Alex when he broke the kiss.

"It's real and it's very powerful. Our hearts long to be together." He looked into her eyes, and she was sure he could see her soul. "We'd both be crazy not to be frightened by it. But we'd also be crazy to walk away from it." He ran his fingers over her moist lips. "Come fly with me, Lara. I promise you'll never regret it." His hand fell away. Then he walked from the room.

Lara closed her eyes and stood motionless until her heart stopped pounding. After a few minutes, she retrieved her towel from the floor and tucked it in her bag. Her hands still trembled. Looping the strap over her shoulder, she headed downstairs.

She and Brett had become friends instantly, almost from the day he started working for her father, before the accident. She'd had a schoolgirl crush on him. She told things to Brett she'd never even told her friends. Half the fun of coming home from school was seeing Brett and telling him all the news.

After the accident, he'd been a lifeline. He was the only bright light in her life, and she'd clung to him. To his credit, he hadn't abandoned her. While other young men enjoyed New York's social scene, Brett spent time with an invalid. Highly unusual. Maybe even suspect.

No. She wouldn't allow Alex's nasty little seed to take root. He was wrong. Brett hadn't used her to gain influence with her father and access to her money. She refused to believe it. Lara's musings brought her to the guesthouse. She paused as she opened the door and heard raised voices.

Across the room, Troy and Brett were faced off.

"I don't care how you justify it," Troy said. "We've missed the mark. Everything Summers said was true. We wanted to create a school for all artists. What we've done is create one that's exclusive."

Brett's sigh was audible to Lara as she stood in the open door. "It'll be the best school in the west…maybe even the world…for young, developing artists."

"For young, affluent artists, Brett. Don't you see the difference? We should have allotted the money for dormitories and consulted a specialist about curriculum. If Sara were alive this wouldn't have happened."

"You're right. It wouldn't. But she's not alive and Daniel won't give us any more money. What should we have sacrificed to hire an education consultant or to build more buildings? The equipment? The beautiful building which you considered so elemental to the artistic environment? Just what would you have changed?" Brett's angry words echoed in the room.

Lara stood frozen to the spot, wishing for all the world she'd not stepped in at just that moment—and wishing even more that she'd left before Brett turned and saw her.

Immediately, the anger left his features.

Seeing his surprise, Troy turned.

Both men shuffled awkwardly as Lara stood within the open doorway.

After a moment, Troy cleared his throat. "You're right. I wouldn't have sacrificed anything. I would have wanted the best of everything. And that, my friend," he said, slapping Brett's shoulder, "is why you're in charge of the money and I'm just the artist.

I'll go see if Eliza needs help for tonight." Tugging his jacket together, he walked toward Lara and kissed her forehead.

"I'm sorry. This was bad timing," she whispered.

"Don't be. He's right. I wouldn't have compromised, and we wouldn't even be this far in the process." He smiled. But his sad little smile made her feel worse.

Suddenly, she hated compromises. Hated settling for second best...in business or in love. After he'd gone, she turned to Brett. "Surely there's a way to find more funds."

Brett shoved his hands in his pockets. "You don't understand, Lara. I'm already out on a limb. I've committed funds your father didn't approve."

Surprise washed through Lara.

Her father was a perfectionist and a strict employer. He demanded total obedience. The Brett she knew would never make a financial move without her father's explicit approval and consent. Why would he risk so much for this project?

Had Troy been so persuasive?

Did Brett believe in this project so much, he was willing to push her father's envelope? Or was he simply that confident in his position at Fallon Enterprises? Alex's insinuations echoed in her thoughts.

"Well," she said, searching for another answer. "It can't be so bad. Surely, there was money for your discretionary use. Dad trusts you."

"Of course, he trusts me. That's why I was able to wire New York and get the money without his signature. Now I have to tell him I spent it."

Lara swallowed hard, thinking about the

implications. Daniel Fallon was not an easy man to defy. To her knowledge, this was the first time Brett had ever questioned her father's authority, let alone bucked it. Still, he was remarkably detached, almost as if he'd already discovered the solution to his problem.

"This week is all about sponsors," she said, probing for the answer. "You can use the money coming in to replace what you took from the account."

"I could have. That's why I approved hiring Summers. I thought if he was as spectacular as everyone said, he'd be a hit and the good will would spill over into our sponsors' donations. But after his little speech this morning, I doubt anyone will drop a dime."

And just a few minutes ago, she had let the "hit of the event" kiss her. Guilt twisted inside her.

At the same time, something about Brett's attitude caught her attention. Something in his tone when he spoke about Alex sounded bitter or sarcastic, not like Brett at all. But then, Brett had responded strangely to Alex from their first encounter this morning. Had they met before and not gotten along? Or worse, had he seen her and Alex together and witnessed the attraction exploding between them?

She waited for Brett to say something more...anything.

But he stood facing the window, almost as if he'd forgotten she was there. He was incredibly calm for a man whose career might be on the line...as if he really didn't believe anything bad would happen. Maybe he didn't. Maybe he believed Daniel Fallon would never take punitive action against a man who was to be his son-in-law.

Suddenly, Lara was sick inside. Unable to face

Brett with her doubts or her guilt, she mumbled something about a shower and headed toward her room.

7

Lara halted her pacing by the dance room window and glanced one more time at her watch. Nine thirty.

Christy was half an hour late.

Lara should have expected it, did expect it. But still, disappointment crept through her. Gripping her fingers, she stared out the window. She had to get hold of herself. If she were honest, she had to admit Christy wasn't to blame for her heightened emotions. And it wasn't disappointment. It was fear. Her carefully constructed world was falling apart around her.

Christy had changed.

Eliza and Troy were in serious financial trouble.

Brett, whom she'd always considered a rock of stability, had put his career in jeopardy and was making bad decisions.

All of their actions were so out of character, so unexpected.

Lara felt as if she'd stepped into a grim, fairy tale world. Everything was going off course, out of kilter, and she was desperate to get it back on track. Helping Christy had become so important, she was ready to jump down the girl's throat for being late. It was too much to put on one lonely, frightened child.

Lara was feeling lost and frightened, too. Shaking her head, she took a deep breath to calm herself.

Troy walked away from the house toward the thick brush of the forest at the back. Just as he reached the edge, he paused and looked back. He scanned the whole house, as if searching to see if anyone was watching. His actions were so furtive, so clandestine.

A whisper of unease brushed Lara's senses. She eased back from the window just far enough not to be seen.

Troy stepped into the bush, moving toward the thicker pine trees. At the same time, a flash of white and movement within the bush caught Lara's eye from another direction.

Troy was meeting someone in the trees...someone he didn't want to be seen with, judging by his behavior.

Lara stepped forward, leaning into the window for a better view, but Troy and his partner disappeared out of her sight. She stalked toward her bag, determined to find out who Troy was meeting.

After stuffing the towels inside her bag, she rolled the two mats she'd stretched out on the floor—just in time to hear wheels moving over the tiles in the hallway.

The door opened, and Christy pushed her way into the room.

Lara rose to her feet. She needed to follow Troy, but his daughter sat slumped in her wheelchair, looking as if the weight of the world was on her shoulders.

Christy focused on her lap. "I had a hard time finding something comfortable to wear," she muttered. Her tone wasn't apologetic, but it wasn't belligerent, either.

"I understand," Lara said. "Are you comfortable?"

Christy shrugged.

Lara remembered feeling the same way. After so

much pain, when one's body found a comfortable place, it refused to move. Each step required sheer willpower.

With one last, regretful look toward the window, Lara unrolled the mats she'd put away only seconds earlier. "Can you get out of your chair?"

"Sure. I can do everything. I just get tired really easy."

"Well, maybe that's because you're not using those muscles."

"That's what my mom says." Christy locked the wheels, pushed the footrests back, and stood. Using the chair for support, she eased herself onto the floor.

Lara shoved the chair out of the way. "How long have you been using the chair?"

Christy shrugged. "A month. Maybe two."

Scooting over, Lara gave the girl a warm smile. "I need to feel your arms and legs, so just relax." She slid her hands up and down, gently pressing. Christy's muscles did not appear to have atrophied in the time she'd been using the chair. A good sign. "We're going to start out real easy, Christy. I'll show you the exercise, you'll practice, and then we'll do it together for several counts. How does that sound?"

Another non-committal shrug.

Lara crossed her legs.

Christy had to use her hands to pull both legs close to her body and into place.

The child was stiffer than Lara had anticipated. Lara straightened, placed her hands on opposite sides of her legs and twisted her lower back.

Christy dutifully complied. Her face screwed into a tight frown and sweat popped on her brow. Emotional stress could cause the excruciating swelling and stiffening known to R.A. sufferers as flares.

Lara turned on the CD, but she couldn't seem to distract Christy from her discomfort. After less than a half hour, Lara feared they'd have to call it quits.

A knock on the door caught both their attention.

Alex strode into the room, looking wonderful in a white T-shirt, blue jeans, and tennis shoes. He carried a beautiful, twelve-string guitar. He flashed his incredible grin, oozing vitality and strength.

Christy's face brightened.

Lara was glad for the reprieve.

"I've a favor to ask," he said, crouching down to their level. "I've been trying to work in another room but I'm not having much luck. Since we're all trying something new and challenging, maybe it would help if we worked side by side."

"You're just playing your guitar." Christy asked. "What's so hard?"

"I'm writing a new song, and I can't seem to get it right."

"You mean you just sit down and play?" Christy's eyes widened. "Just like that, you make a song?"

Alex nodded. "It's how I do it."

"But don't you need a computer or maybe even a pen and paper to write it down?"

"Nope. I promise I won't disturb you or interrupt your workout. I'll just sit over there by the window and play."

"I guess it's OK," she said.

"Thanks, ladies." Alex rose. Scooping a chair out of a corner of the room, he placed it in the middle of the bright, sunny window. He tucked the guitar beneath one arm and bent over it. Sharp, discordant sounds came when he plucked at the strings. He continued to strum up and down in scales, and slowly but surely, clear notes wafted in the air. A melody flowed out, but was aborted. He started again, only to come to the same abrupt end. He paused, began with a different tune, a more familiar, popular tune. He cut it short and flowed into the same original melody, which stopped at the same place. He looked up, saw them watching him and leaned forward, resting his arm on the guitar. With a slight smile, he said, "I won't disturb you, if you won't disturb me."

Lara turned her back to Alex and wiggled her eyebrows in an "Oh, brother" expression.

Christy giggled.

Lara launched into the workout routine.

As she worked, Christy stole glances over Lara's shoulder. She relaxed with Alex's music and her movements came easier. Soon she was flowing from one effort to the next without the winces of pain.

Lara noted it, but said nothing.

Leaning forward, Christy whispered, "Listen to the song."

Lara listened.

Alex played low, pulsating chords with Lara's movements and high pitched ones with Christy's exercises. When they worked together, the tones blended into a rhythmic melody.

"It sounds like us, doesn't it? Do you think he's making a song about us?" Christy whispered.

"It wouldn't surprise me," Lara replied.

Awed, Christy unabashedly watched Alex. She slipped thoughtlessly from movement to movement, swaying to the tune. Intent on the song, Christy didn't seem to realize what she was doing.

After a while, Lara called a halt to the workout.

"Already?" Christy asked, turning to Lara with obvious surprise.

"We've been doing this for an hour and a half. I don't want to wear you out on our first day together."

"I've been moving for an hour and a half?"

Lara nodded. "How do you feel? Are you tired?"

"I feel—" Christy stared at her blankly.

Lara rose to her feet and then pulled Christy up.

The younger girl looked at Lara. A slow smile crawled over her lips. "I did it, didn't I?"

Lara returned the smile. "Yes, you did."

Christy motioned toward Alex with her head. "Did you plan this with him?" she whispered.

"I didn't want an audience anymore than you did."

"You got that right. I think *we* were the entertainment," Christy replied.

Lara placed a hand on her shoulder and squeezed. "All I know is it worked."

Christy burst into a brilliant smile. "Yeah, it worked."

Alex had stopped playing.

Christy turned to him. "I think since we get along so well together when we work, we should relax together, too."

He rose, stretching his long body as he stood. "I could use a little relaxation. What did you have in mind?"

"My nurse will make me spend at least an hour in the spa. You guys could come with me. It's a part of the pool, and it looks down on the valley. It's really cool."

Alex smiled. "As cool as my music?"

Laughing, Christy shook her head. "That's way

cool. The pool's just neat."

He lifted the guitar. "Let me put this away, and I'll meet you in ten minutes."

Christy turned to Lara. "How long will it take you?"

Lara dug in her bag. "I won't be able to come, Christy. I've got some things I need to do."

"Aw, come on, Lara. We have to celebrate. You can come for a half hour, can't you?"

"I don't have a swimsuit," Lara said, barely above a whisper.

"Oh, is that all?" Christy grinned. "Don't worry. Mom's always got extras around in different sizes. She does it on purpose." Christy's exuberant expression faded. "Oh, Lara, I'm sorry. I forgot you don't wear swimsuits because of the scars."

Alex had crossed the room by now and stood beside Christy. "What scars?"

Lara didn't answer, couldn't meet his gaze. She fiddled with her towel, wrapping it around her neck.

"On her legs, from all of her surgeries." Christy had no qualms about filling him in. "She says they're everywhere and look really bad."

"Ahhh," he said in a quiet voice. "I'd forgotten."

There was a short, stilted pause.

Lara didn't dare look at Alex.

"But didn't we already decide what's on the inside is more important? What's a few scars between friends?"

The last time she'd used a towel to brush off the perspiration, he'd taken it and tenderly wiped it across her skin. His gaze said he'd like to do it again.

At the memory of his touch, a slow burn kindled somewhere deep inside her. Her fingertips started to tingle, and her face flushed warm. She wanted to step into his embrace and let the fire consume her. Confused, she dropped the towel into the open bag and propped her hands on her hips. She needed a few seconds to regain control. Taking a breath, she turned to Christy. "The scars aren't important." She hoped she sounded more confident than she felt. "And if I hadn't already promised Brett I'd meet him at the school, I'd love to sit in the spa with you."

"Brett can't wait a little while?"

"Brett and I have been waiting quite a while to be together, don't you think, Christy?"

"Yeah, I guess that's true. Can we do it tomorrow?"

Lara nodded.

Christy gave her a quick hug, and then headed for her wheelchair. Instead of sitting in it, she grabbed it by the handles and walked to the door.

Alex held the door open while she went through. With one last glance at Lara, he followed, closing the door. She could hear them talking as they walked down the hall.

She zipped her bag, wrapped her skirt around her waist and slid the bag strap onto her shoulder. She might still find Troy. She hurried down the winding staircase toward the front door.

Two guards in black suits stood outside La Guitarra's room.

She nodded a greeting as she passed. Behind her, the door opened. She glanced back to see Alex step out.

Obviously, all of the valuable guitars were stored in the same room.

Alex said something to the guards and followed Lara out into the bright sunlight. "You know," he said as they walked down the steps toward the guesthouses. "You don't have to do that."

She glanced sideways, barely pausing. "Do what?"

"Take Brett out of your bag and flash him in front of you like a shield. I promise I won't do anything else to make you uncomfortable."

"I don't use him like a shield."

"Yes, you do. Every time I get too close, you talk about Brett to remind me about him. Or maybe you're reminding yourself." He studied her as they walked together. "That's it, isn't it? You're reminding yourself, arming yourself against my intense appeal." He said it in a joking tone.

But he was so close to the truth, she couldn't smile at his teasing.

They walked a few steps more before he touched her arm. "Lara?"

She didn't want to stop, didn't want to give him the opportunity to wear down her resistance. Gritting her teeth, she turned to face him.

"I don't want to get in the way of your relationship with Christy. If you want to meet her in the spa, I'll make some excuse."

"Oh no, that would be too easy. You're not going to get off the hook."

"Off the hook? I was offering to let you have all the fun."

"Is it fun, Alex? Do you really want to spend the afternoon with a rebellious kid you barely know or are you just using her to get at me?"

He leaned back as if he'd been struck. "Did I commit a crime you forgot to tell me about? When did I become the bad guy?"

Irritated, Lara glanced at the side of the house. The

longer she dallied with Alex, the less likely she would find Troy. Still she needed to settle things with Alex. She straightened and faced him. "From the beginning. All the signs were there, I just didn't pay attention."

"What signs? Oh...I get it. You mean you should have listened to the gossip."

"Paid attention to the signs, Alex. First of all, you waltzed in here and sabotaged my mother's school. You've made continuous advances even after I said no. Then you add insult to injury by questioning Brett's motives."

"I see."

"What do you see?"

"I only stated the obvious about the school, Lara. The real reason you're angry with me is because my suggestion about Brett struck a raw nerve."

Lara gripped her shoulder strap and met his gaze squarely. "The point is, you have no right questioning anyone else's motives when you have your own past as an example."

"Finally, we get to the real issue. You've heard the gossip about the Comtessa."

"I'm not fishing for information about your private life. I just don't think you should be intruding into mine."

He folded his arms. "Point taken. I overstepped the polite bounds, but in my defense, I was compelled. Quite honestly, Lara, I saw something special in you."

"And it doesn't matter to you that I have an understanding with someone else."

"As far as I can see there's not much of anything going on between you and Fraser, let alone an understanding. It seems more like what everyone else expects to happen. Has he made promises?"

She spun away. "Of course not. Brett would never falsely lead me on." Lara's own words penetrated her angry refusal. They were true, of course. Brett wouldn't hurt her in any way. But he'd never spoken any promises, any words of commitment. Their "understanding" had always been her wishful thinking. Her girlhood dreams brought them together...and Brett had never had the courage to tell her no.

Not until this morning. With their frustrated exchange fresh in her mind, Lara could no longer deny the indications.

Had her arrival, with her childish dreams and everyone's expectations, created the tension in Brett? She had to speak to him, to sort this out.

How was Alex able to know her so thoroughly while he remained a great, beckoning mystery?

"That's an unfair judgment on someone you don't know...especially when your reputation isn't pristine."

"We're back to the Comtessa."

Exasperated, she recognized the waspish quality of her tone. "All right, we are. She's managed your career. You've used her money for support."

"Of course. It's her obligation."

Lara sputtered to a halt. Speechless, she stared at him.

"The Comtessa is my mother, Lara. She remarried and took another name, but continued to manage my career with the same proprietary interest. People misinterpreted her motives. I'm not quite certain how the sordid rumor got started, but it did. She swears my father started it in an attempt to humiliate her and drive a wedge between us."

Stunned, Lara murmured, "But you didn't let him

succeed?"

"I don't believe he even tried. He wouldn't have spent that much time on either my mother, or me."

His words mimicked the same words Rupert Townsend had used when talking about her father. "I guess there's been gossip about my father as well."

He shook his head. "I told you. I don't waste time on gossip, but I do recognize the kinship between us. That wasn't a lie." His words were too raw, too close to the truth.

She wanted to turn away, but he grasped her arms and held her still.

"Tell me you don't feel it too, Lara." He gave her a little shake, forcing her to meet his gaze. "If you tell me you feel absolutely nothing, I'll walk away right now and never bother you again."

Lara sagged into his grip. "I can't deny it, Alex. I feel it, but I have questions. You said you wanted only honesty between us so here it is. I don't trust the kinship between us. You waltz into my life and know things about me a stranger wouldn't know, almost as if you've made a study of me. You're trying to drive a wedge between me and my...friend and you say things that make me feel wonderful and incredibly special. But I'm not. All women are special to you...and most of them are wealthy. I'm an heiress, Alex. I have to be suspicious."

Alex's features hardened, and he looked away. In a momentary flash, she wondered if she was reading frustration or calculation. Lara couldn't tell, and it only added to her confusion.

When he turned back, his face was blank. "I know what it is to be wanted for something that has nothing to do with who you are, Lara. That's why I asked for honesty between us."

She laughed out loud. "You said so, and then promptly did everything you could do to be different and create mystery around yourself."

Alex smiled his slow, knowing smile. "But it is the real me, Lara. Unpredictable. Free. It's the life I've chosen for myself. The one I try to keep from my fans and the one I think you're dying to live."

"How can I be dying to live it when I don't even understand it?"

"What don't you understand? Ask me anything. I'll try to explain."

Lara hesitated. What exactly had he done…except make her feel like a woman? Was the real problem that she didn't trust Alex or her own sensuality? She needed to know the truth.

Lara had to demystify Alex's compelling attraction. A few feet away, just off the path, a marble bench rested beneath an Arizona willow. Lara walked toward it and sat down. Alex joined her as she let her bag slide from her shoulder to the ground.

"Why didn't you stop the rumors about your mother? They were ugly and obviously upset her."

"When the rumors first started, my mother had earned her reputation. She was bitter and demanding. She was determined to control me as she had never been able to control my father. I was young and too inexperienced to check her efforts." His jaw hardened and he paused, but only for a moment. "Eventually, we worked things out. By that time, the rumors served another purpose. I allowed my mother to handle the image of Alejandro Summers because it left me free to be Alex, student and eventually professor. The rumors kept away certain kinds of females."

"What kind?"

"Mamas and their daughters. The ones in love with the myth, who knew nothing about the real man. The ones who wanted to keep the myth for their own, to take it out, and show it off when company comes to visit. I don't fit into a cage very well."

"Is that what you think a relationship is? A cage?"

"All relationships are cages, especially the legal institution called marriage. Most relationships are a way of controlling the people you supposedly care about."

Lara studied him, thinking he must have been hurt very badly. "Was it your mother or someone else who taught you that lesson?" she asked.

He stared at a distant spot, his legs stretched out as he leaned back on the bench. His torso was long and lean…so touchable.

Lara could easily understand why women wanted to hold him and keep him. She had to turn away to keep from reaching out.

"Does it matter?" he asked after a while.

"Yes, I think so. If that's how you feel, I can't imagine why you'd be interested in a relationship with me. Because that's what it would be with me. I'm definitely not interested in anything else."

A smile tugged at the corners of his mouth. "Our friendship would be based on kinship and mutual respect for each other's freedom." That smile. If he could bottle it or put it in a package and sell it, he'd have a million more fans.

Lara felt her resistance slipping and yet he'd done little more than sit beside her and talk. "You assume a lot about me," she said. "How do you know I wouldn't want to keep you in a cage?" *How do you know, once that smile and long, taut body belonged to me, I'd ever let it go?*

He leaned forward, inches from her face. "I know once you've tasted freedom as I have, you'll respect it. You would never try to control someone else as you've been controlled."

"I haven't been…" Lara halted. His dark eyes were so close, so piercing. They reached inside her and uncovered the lie even before she finished it. Hiding behind illusions was impossible with him only a breath away.

She had always been loved, always known her parents' deep and abiding commitment to her. She felt so much a part of their lives, she found it difficult to identify with Alex's emotional distance from his parents. But she had to acknowledge that with her parents' abiding love had come control. Her father's expectations. Her mother's rigid dictates. For as long as she could remember things had been demanded from her…gently and lovingly expressed, but demands nonetheless. Comportment. Grace. Conformity. Nothing less was acceptable. When her mother was taken so unexpectedly, Lara had felt cast adrift, rudderless. If her mother had lived, perhaps Lara would have matured on her own, pulled away from the rigid dictates. Instead, she had mourned and yearned for that safe, familiar environment.

Rupert Townsend had referred to it and Eliza had tried to talk about it, but it had taken Alex's piercing honesty to make Lara see it. That he should know, should say the words that had been swimming inside her, unsaid, unacknowledged, made her want to weep. She didn't know whether to thank him or to be angry with him for once again forcing himself into her privacy.

He was a breath away. His eyes were dark and caressing and full of compassion.

She wanted him to kiss her.

But he didn't.

Lara ached with the need to feel his arms around her. She was a twenty-four-year-old virgin, overripe, naïve, and more than anxious to be whole.

Alex would make her transition into womanhood easy. With his powerful touch, musical voice and knowing ways, he would make it wonderful. Maybe even glorious.

She leaned forward, hoping he would take the hint.

His jaw tightened with tension, but he never moved.

And suddenly she understood.

He wouldn't use this moment to seduce her even though he was quite capable of doing so. He was allowing her the freedom to choose for herself, to be in control of her own life.

Right now, she hated him for it.

Why wouldn't he just sweep her into his arms and kiss her until she couldn't think anymore? That would be so much more like a fairy tale. Lara closed her eyes. What was wrong with her?

Somewhere behind the house, a door slammed.

Christy was waiting for Alex, and reality rushed back to Lara. She was sitting on a park bench in the open. Anyone in the house or on the grounds could see them. Suddenly flustered, Lara reached for her bag. "I…I have to meet Brett."

Alex rose slowly to his feet, a wry smile on his lips.

"I'm not using him as a shield," Lara said when she saw the smile. "I'm just late."

"Then by all means, hurry." He gestured down the walkway in a mocking manner.

Clutching her bag, Lara strode away.

~*~

Alex noted that she didn't have the courage to look back. He stood a moment more, wondering at the game he played. Lara Fallon should be off limits. He didn't have time to indulge in his bizarre fascination for forbidden fruit. But he couldn't seem to help himself.

The attraction between them was real, like wildfire. Everything he'd said to her about how he felt was true. He wasn't lying. He had simply left out some information that didn't need to be shared. So why did he feel so guilty every time she walked away? If he had his way, Lara wouldn't go. She'd stay and what would happen between them would be consuming, important, maybe even life changing. But it would be tainted by what he had left out.

The only way to prevent that from happening was to get to the bottom of the mystery with the directors of the Fallon School of Art. It was proving to be a difficult task.

When Lara had entered the guesthouse, he made his way around the corner to the back of the main house. While playing his guitar at the window, he'd seen Troy leave the forest...and he'd seen Lara's glance stray to this corner once too often. Obviously, she'd seen Troy as well. What was the man up to? And what part did Lara play?

He had to check it out.

At the edge of the forest, he found Troy's

footprints and tracked them into the softer soil of the bush. A few yards in, behind a stand of short, stubby pines, Alex found another set of prints. Troy met someone then retraced his steps alone.

So where had his partner come from?

Alex followed the other footsteps along a path edging the forest. They led him around the house toward the rest of the complex, and ended abruptly at the edge of the gravel between the two guesthouses. Alex's gaze swept over the empty complex. Not a soul in sight. No gardeners or grounds men, no security men, not even a maid, who—considering the time— should have been making her way toward the guesthouses. No one was in sight. The trail was cold.

Gritting his teeth, Alex studied the footsteps. Large. Definitely a man's...and they ended precisely between the two guesthouses. Was it because the guesthouses provided cover to leave or because one of the guesthouses was the destination?

Only three people, besides himself, occupied those guesthouses. Lara, Fraser, and Carlos. Fraser had ample opportunity to speak with Troy alone. They didn't need to have clandestine meetings in the forest. And Lara had been with Alex all morning.

So that left Carlos. But what connection did Carlos have with Southwest pottery or even with Troy Madrigal? It didn't make sense.

Shaking his head, Alex stepped onto the gravel and headed toward his bungalow to change. The deeper he got into this, the less he knew. The simple task UNESCO had set before him was turning into a tangled web, especially since it had the potential to destroy what could be the first meaningful relationship he'd had in years.

~*~

Lara called her driver upon entering the guesthouse. By the time he arrived, she'd showered and slipped into jeans, T-shirt, and tennis shoes. Not giving herself time to think, she pulled her hair into a tiny ponytail, grabbed a sweatshirt and headed out the door.

When she arrived at the school, Troy was already there. He greeted her with a warm smile and a kiss on the cheek, as if nothing were out of the ordinary.

Brett was stressing, drowning in last-minute details.

Troy had brought a picnic lunch from the house, and had been trying to get the younger man to slow down and eat but he'd resisted until Lara arrived, and even then, his capitulation was decidedly grudging.

The three of them sat on the large overstuffed sofas of the meeting room and enjoyed cold-cut sandwiches put together by Troy's cook. Their conversation centered around the last grand celebration of the week, a cocktail party at the school.

Brett and Troy had been screening student's applications for months and had narrowed the field down to fifty young applicants. The upcoming dinner was designed to showcase the applicants attending and to present donor appreciation plaques, which would be displayed on the school's common room wall. The opportunity for one final bid for money would also take place.

A tremendous amount of work still needed to be done before the event. Listening, Lara volunteered to help with the filing, mailing, and sorting of the paperwork.

She headed down the hall to Brett's office. Just as she opened the first file, Brett cursed. Lara hurried to the room from which the men's voices now emanated. She found them intensely examining the contents of several boxes.

Troy paused just long enough to gesture to the crates. "The donor plaques have arrived, and they're all wrong. We'll have to proof all the errors and return them to Flagstaff today in order for them to be ready by Saturday." He sighed. "And their business office closes at five."

Lara glanced at her watch. "Only three hours away."

"Don't forget the drive. It'll take half an hour to get there and we've only just begun," Brett said.

"Give me a list of donors, and I'll start comparing names and spellings."

Soon, Lara was immersed in lists. She made better time than either of the men. Within an hour, she was compiling her list with Brett's and Troy's as they loaded the boxes into Troy's car. Lara suggested Brett go with him.

"I have piles of applicants to sort through still," he said.

"I can sort. Just give me the criteria," Lara offered.

Troy agreed. "I'd feel better if we both handled this. We can't afford another mistake."

Brett gave Lara a quick walk-through of the process while Troy locked down the facility. Then Troy showed her how to arm the building's security.

Lara stood at the entrance and waved goodbye. Back inside, she poured a cup of tea, then settled comfortably behind Brett's desk and started sorting.

The primary qualification for the school was the ability to afford the substantial tuition.

Alex was right.

The pile of qualified applicants lagged behind the unqualified.

One application came from the parents of an autistic son. They'd sent photos, which all started in a blurred world. The images were smudged as if seen through a dirty lens. Then one object would come clear. Two or three objects in the picture would be perfect and from those pieces, the subject could be determined. One was a picture of children playing in the park. Another was a classroom and a city street.

Lara was seeing the world as this autistic child saw it.

The parents were certainly not able to afford the school's tuition.

Lara tossed the application into the discard pile.

The next discards were a young Native American boy who worked with clay, and a teenage girl who sang opera like a diva, but sat in a wheelchair.

The more Lara worked, the more discouraged she became.

The criteria for the school had been established long before, probably when her mother was still alive…her idea, her dream. As a patron of the arts, she would have been most concerned with the quality of the work.

Lara couldn't help but think about Christy. The happiness in the girl's eyes when she completed the workout earlier that day was worth a thousand dollars. What would it be like to give these children the same opportunity to succeed? When the last application was finally sorted, she stared at the large stack of discards, hurting over the fact that behind each one was a child worthy of help.

But what could she do?

Brett had already over-committed funds and refused to budge on this issue. Her father would never approve more money for dormitories and besides, most of these children would need supervision of some sort. That meant additional personnel, wages, benefits.

Alex had been unequivocally correct. The Fallon School of Art was an exclusive facility for rich children...not for needy ones.

And she could do nothing about it. She couldn't even be responsible for her own future. Frustrated, she shoved the applications aside and leaned forward on the desk.

In front of her was Brett's large, leather-bound check ledger. Helpless and frustrated, she flipped open the cover and thumbed the pages. Staring at the edge of the sheets, laying one on top of the other, she noticed a space, as if a page were missing.

Curious, she slid her nail into the space and lifted the pages. It appeared an entire sheet, three checks in all, had been torn out of the book with their carbon sheet. Lara checked the numbers on the previous page and the one after to verify the number sequence. The ledger was definitely missing the three checks and their carbon.

Lara wrote a note to leave on Brett's desk, and then decided against it. A message about missing checks was not one she should leave lying around.

Just as she threw it into the trash, she heard someone at the door. Time had flown by. Her driver must have returned to pick her up. Shutting off the lights in the office, she locked the building and set the alarm.

She'd not had the chance to speak with Brett about their relationship. Now she needed to discuss two things with him—where they were going as a couple, and the missing checks.

8

Lara twirled her champagne glass by its stem and tried very hard not to look bored as Rupert Townsend expounded on the beauty of modern décor. According to him, the smooth, pure lines were perfect for the desert landscape. His home in Oak Creek Canyon was a perfect example and she would have to come and see.

Not if I have to listen to you for hours on end. She'd been listening to Rupert almost since they'd arrived at the small French restaurant.

Eliza had rented the establishment for a dinner party of thirty or so…the select few.

The minute Rupert saw Lara standing on the small balcony over the ravine, he'd made his way to her side.

Had her mother ever really been attracted to this self-absorbed man? Or was it the other way around? Was he so attracted to her he'd spent a lifetime loving her from afar? Lara looked at him, wondering what he'd been like as a young man.

"And just what is that look all about, missy?"

He was too sharp. Caught red-handed, she decided honesty was the best policy.

"I was wondering what you looked like when you were younger," she said.

"What on earth led to this line of thought?"

Lara twirled her glass. "You and my mother," she said rather bluntly.

All the belligerent posturing fled from his features.

"I see," he said in a low voice. "You do cut to the chase, don't you?"

"I'm not as good at socializing as my mother."

Townsend slanted her a look. "What is it you want to know about us?"

Lara walked to edge of the patio. The balcony extended over a small but deep ravine with a stream at the bottom. She looked down on the tops of trees and shrubs growing at the stream's edge. Light reflected off the patio into the dark swirls of brush, and she could hear the gurgle of water. She set her glass on the flat, wooden top rail and turned back to Rupert. "I don't want to know anything about the past. I just want to know why you're here."

Rupert twirled his own bourbon glass as a wry smile slipped over his features. "It's the social event of the season."

She shook her head. "You've been mocking it since you arrived. And as far as I can tell, you're not here to invest, so why did you come?"

"Do you really want to know?" he asked, fixing his gaze on her.

"I think I already do. I think you came to see how badly my father would screw up my mother's dream."

One of his eyebrows rose before he sipped his drink. "You're much more perceptive than you pretend, little Lara."

She shrugged and turned away. Leaning on the railing, she peered into the dark crevasse in front of her.

Rupert stood beside her, his hand in his pocket and his drink held before him like a shield. "I take it you don't approve of my reasons for being here."

"My approval or disapproval doesn't matter. I just

don't see the point. My mother is gone. It doesn't matter to her one way or another and I assure you, Mr. Townsend, your gloating is not impacting my father. So what's the point?"

"Not only are you perceptive but you have claws." He sighed heavily. "I'd like to think something that means so much to me would affect your father in some way."

"My father is a very self-contained man. The only person who could ever reach him was my mother. Now that she's gone, very little touches him. If I've come to accept that fact, you should be able to."

For the first time, Lara saw a softness in his gaze. "Has it been very hard being his daughter?"

Lara met his sympathetic look squarely. "At times, it was harder being my mother's daughter." She'd shocked him.

He'd clearly placed Sara Fallon on a pedestal for so long, he wasn't willing to see her any other way.

Lara gripped her glass and leaned against the rail. "That's all in the past," she said. "What really matters now are the things she left behind. Her love for us, and her dream of a school to help children. It's a good thing. My father is supporting her dream because he loved her. Doing it helps him to get through the days."

"And you think I should do the same, turn my negative focus to a positive one and support the school?"

She shrugged. "If you cared for my mother as much as you say, it would seem only natural. You love art. So many children will grow up to create beautiful things for the world. And it bears the name of a woman you loved. How can you not support it?"

His wry smile returned as he studied his swirling

bourbon glass. "You're a clever, clever little cat, Lara," he said in a quiet voice. "Consider me sufficiently chastised…and in spite of what you think, you're very much like your mother." Bending, he kissed her forehead and wandered away.

Had it worked? Would he invest? She had no way of knowing. But she had discovered something. Most of what she'd said to Rupert applied to her. The people she loved were in trouble. Her mother's dream was falling apart. She couldn't just stand by and watch it happen. This patio was full of her mother's friends— many of whom were holding out. She intended to see those deep pockets emptied.

Needing strength to do something foreign to her, she took a deep breath, set her champagne glass on the tray of a passing waiter, and headed for a group of businessmen. They were friends of her father's, who'd somehow managed to take time out of their schedules to attend…unlike him. For the moment, Lara refused to dwell on the issue, but she couldn't ignore the fact that her father's influence would have brought his friends around much better than hers.

At first, the conversation was stilted. All of her energy went into appearing bright and unconcerned. But she was determined to give it her best shot, and soon, a few of them loosened up. One or two finally admitted their concerns about the school.

Brett was right.

Alex's little speech had made the rounds.

People were questioning the direction and focus of the school.

Lara repeated what Brett had said about starts and stops with any new project. But wasn't it wonderful they'd discovered the problem early enough to fix it?

With an enigmatic smile, she left her words hanging in the air, as if a solution were already in the works. Nodding, she moved on to the next group. It became her modus operandi, and it created a stir.

Were people more surprised by what she said, or the fact that overnight, Sara's quiet daughter had suddenly developed personality?

By the time dinner was served, Lara was exhausted. Keeping the smile on her face was all she could manage. She sat in front of her place card at the table and waited for Brett, Eliza, and Troy. Troy and Eliza finally joined her, but not before she'd drained almost a full glass of water.

The small dining room was designed with a French cottage motif. A fire crackled in the stone fireplace, mauve-colored cabbage rose patterns adorned all the chairs and curtains, and fresh cut flowers filled numerous vases. Crystal and fine china sparkled on the tables, and the smells from the kitchen made Lara hungry.

Brett was still making the rounds as the waiter set a small salad in front of Lara.

Eliza stepped to the fireplace and made a short welcoming speech, and then invited everyone to begin eating.

Brett eased into the seat beside Lara...almost as if he'd been waiting for dinner to start.

She glanced at him, questions niggling at her mind. Was he avoiding her, or was she being overly sensitive?

As he bent over to scoot his chair forward, he whispered, "What on earth did you say to Rupert Townsend? He just offered me three hundred thousand dollars for the school and said I could thank you."

Eliza made a small sound, and Troy froze with his fork in mid-air.

"Lara," Eliza whispered. "What *did* you say?"

Uncomfortable, Lara picked at her salad. "Actually, I gave him a lecture about being a negative influence and told him to spend his time better."

"You didn't!" Eliza started to giggle.

"Someone should have been honest with him a long time ago," she replied.

Eliza continued to laugh.

Troy smiled.

Brett shook his head. "You took a chance, Lara. It could have backfired. He could have left the event."

Frowning, Lara stared at Brett. "But it didn't. It worked and now we have the money."

"Well, yes, but it could have been disastrous."

Exasperated, Lara shoved her salad around the plate. "Someone had to do something, Brett." She hesitated, but only for a moment. "And while we're at it, you might as well know, I've talked it around that we have a solution to the curriculum problem on everyone's mind."

"You did what?"

"I hinted we have a solution."

"You know we don't."

His attitude put her over the edge.

"Well, why don't we?" she asked in a firm, low voice. "We have a multi-million dollar project and two years of work teetering on the brink of failure and instead of finding a solution, we're crying 'woe is me' and throwing up our hands."

Even in the soft firelight, she could see Brett's jaw clench. "I told you why."

Lara drew her breath. "Well, I don't buy it. My father won't stand by and see his money thrown away. He wants this school to be successful, and he'd be stupid not to forgive just about any mistake if a solution came with it."

"Lara, you shouldn't be meddling in this. You don't understand everything that's going on."

"Then tell me what is going on, Brett, so I won't make mistakes."

He didn't respond.

Her words hung in the air.

Brett's gaze darted toward Eliza and Troy.

Lara's dropped to the table.

The waiter came for her salad, and she let it go without having tasted a bite. She stared at the Chicken Cordon Bleu he placed in front of her.

"I think you're right, Lara," Troy said. "We've all been working so hard, we've let these last few hurdles overcome us."

"I still can't get over Rupert," Eliza said. "You're probably the only person in the world he'd let talk to him like that."

"I'm Sara's daughter. It makes sense," she said with a half smile. The awkward moment passed, but not the discomfort. She nibbled at her chicken.

Brett reached for his glass. Apparently, he'd expected her to sit on her hands and pretend nothing was happening. Or did he just want her to stay out of it? Was he afraid she might discover something he didn't want her to know? Lara placed her fork on her plate and let her hand drop to her lap.

Eliza said something about the chicken, and Lara made an appropriate reply.

As a creamy chocolate mousse was served, a

waiter approached Brett and whispered to him. Brett excused himself.

Lara watched him go, wondering what could be so important to keep pulling him away.

Eliza rose. "I think it's time we got this road trip on the road," she said with a smile. "Ladies and gentlemen," she said, addressing the small gathering. The firelight glinted off her hair and splashes of burnt orange and red reflected from the silk scarf at her neck. "As many of you know, some of the shop owners of Tlaquepaque Village have kept their doors open for us this evening. The village contains specialty shops and galleries I think you'll find very interesting. One shop owner has a box of Havana cigars in stock and a blend of pipe tobacco just arrived from England. He's holding samples for those of you who might be interested. Also, there's a special treat in the central plaza. So if you'll join me, we'll take the short stroll across the way."

Lara stood and buttoned her long black jacket over the matching slacks she'd chosen to wear. She'd discovered evenings in the desert were as crisp and cold as winter evenings anywhere else. Her first night with the balmy weather had been an exception. The fact that there were balmy nights in the middle of winter still enchanted her. Above her, the sky was ebony and velvet. The stars were clear, crisp and sparkled like diamonds.

Milly Johansson broke away from her husband's entourage and came toward her.

Lara stifled a groan. She wasn't up to hearing more of Milly's comments but at the same time, she couldn't bear to hurt her feelings. There was something vulnerable about Milly that made Lara stand still and greet her with a smile.

"Hello," Milly said in a quiet voice. "I wanted to let you know we're not going to invest...at least not yet."

Lara's heart sank. "I'm sorry to hear that, Milly. Did your prayers tell you to do this, or are you concerned about the school's direction?"

Milly shook her head. "My prayers have the most to do with it." She stood for a few moments, her dark gaze uncertain and hesitant.

"So you've heard more bad news about me?"

Milly nodded again.

Lara laughed. "Trust me, Milly, all I've had since I got here is bad news. Nothing you can say will upset me any more than I already am."

"You don't understand," Milly said with a shake of her head. "You're headed for danger."

Lara paused. A tingling started at her fingertips. She tried to play her reaction down. "And I'm going to meet a tall, dark stranger who will save me. Remember, I went to a fortune teller when I was fourteen."

"You've already met him," Milly said without pause. "You know he's come to change your life and you know you must make a decision. But you're confused, and danger is building all around you. It will make your decisions even more difficult."

Lara swallowed, trying hard not to show her discomfort. "If he's the tall, dark stranger like in a romance, he can save me."

Milly shook his head. "He can help you, but you have to save yourself, Lara. You have to decide who you are and what you must do."

Lara's joking attitude fled. "Milly, maybe you can

make sense of all this, but it's too mysterious and confusing for me. I'm starting to get a little scared."

Milly sighed heavily. "I know. This is how things come to me, in bits and pieces and cloudy. Sometimes it's more trouble than help. I'm not a very capable messenger. But it's always true. So I've learned to just listen to the promptings of the Holy Spirit, to listen and wait until it all makes sense. I've learned to go with the flow."

Lara smiled. "Someone else has been telling me I need to do the same thing."

"He's right. You have to listen to him."

Lara halted. "I didn't say it was a him."

Milly shrugged. "But it is. I wish I could tell you something to help you understand. Perhaps now you would pray with me."

Lara paused and stared off into space. She hadn't prayed since she'd arrived. Hadn't asked for God's guidance once, not even when she'd been most tempted by Alex's kisses, or just a few minutes ago when she needed to face her father's friends. She'd forgotten Him, but He had not forgotten her. "I think that's the best idea I've heard all night."

Milly smiled her sweet, shy smile and grasped Lara's hands. Almost immediately Lara felt heat emanating from Milly's fingers—a comforting warmth...as if Jesus himself had taken her hands to soothe her fears.

"Lord," Milly began. "We ask you to open Lara's heart and mind to Your path for her. We ask You to give her discernment in the days ahead and most of all, to protect and guide her." Milly ended the prayer, released Lara, and then stepped back. "I feel better now. I know you have some help."

Avery Johansson called to his wife as the group headed in the direction of a limousine parked at the curb. "I have to go. We leave for L.A. tomorrow for a recording session," Milly said. "We're flying out early." She grasped Lara's hand. "You've come to Sedona for a reason, Lara. Let Him guide you and strengthen you. You'll know what to do when the time is right." With another of her soft, shy smiles, she turned and followed her husband.

He wrapped an arm protectively around her as he led her back to the car. As he helped Milly in, he turned back to Lara and waved once, almost as if to reassure her.

Lara stood in stunned silence even after they had gone. Danger and trust. Decisions coming out of indecision. Far too mystical to follow, and yet…somehow she was beginning to believe. From the moment she'd stood on the balcony and watched the Sedona sunset, she'd felt different, touched by God. Was she really headed for danger? Did the future of the school depend on what she did?

Not if Brett had anything to do with it. He was determined to keep her out of it.

But she was the only one doing anything about their current problems. It didn't make any sense. Shivering, she tugged her coat tight. Across the street, Rupert Townsend walked toward the shopping village. His taciturn, no-nonsense nature could help her get back on firm ground. She hurried ahead to loop her arm through his. "Thank you," she said in a quiet voice.

The older man turned slightly before laying his hand over hers.

"Sometimes even wise old men need a challenge

or two."

Lara shook her head. "It's funny. Everyone seems to be telling me the same things these days. Someone else just told me life should be full of challenges and change."

"Really? Sounds like an interesting person. Anyone I know?"

Lara slanted a look at Rupert. "Perhaps you know him."

She said nothing more and Rupert laughed. "Lara, Lara. You know my most intimate secret, but won't even hint at one of yours."

"I have no secrets," she replied.

"Now that, my dear, is a shame. A woman like you should have many secrets." Rupert Townsend was too clever, intuitive.

If she said any more, he might just put two and two together. But maybe it wouldn't be a bad thing. Maybe what she needed was someone to talk to. She studied his profile in silence. Could she trust him? She had such a hard time placing confidence in anyone but her closest family friends, and now even their motives were called into question. How could she rely on Rupert Townsend to keep her secrets? She couldn't.

Milly was right. Lara needed to find the truth for herself, to rely on her own instincts. Gripping Rupert's arm, Lara walked toward the entrance to the shops.

Tlaquepaque Village was of Spanish colonial design, complete with enclosing six-foot walls. Wrought iron balconies extended beyond wooden shutter doors. Ivy covered rounded archways, stucco walls studded with wood, and hand-painted tiles completed the picture. A thousand tiny white lights lit the complex from the Christmas season just passed.

They entered a broad central plaza. The lights from the surrounding shop doors spilled like golden streams into the darkened area. Freestanding wrought iron fireplaces crackled and snapped with warm flames, creating a welcome glow over the plaza.

Outside one shop, small tables and chairs were situated close to a fire stand. People were already seated in them and telltale whispers of smoke floated up into the night sky. The scent of pipe tobacco wafted toward Lara and her companion.

Rupert took a deep breath. "Mmmm. It's been a long time since I've enjoyed that scent. I just might break my doctor's orders tonight."

"Life is about challenges," Lara said with a smile.

As they approached the group, something caught Lara's eye. Guards in black suits stood on each side of the central water fountain. Eliza had said something about a surprise.

Lara's stomach clenched. She rounded the corner and spotted two stools in front of the tobacco shop. She stopped, but not soon enough. Alex and Carlos emerged from the shadows behind the fountain and took their seats on the stools. Alex carried La Guitarra.

Panic shot through Lara. Here she was, beneath a sky shot with brilliant stars, so close she could almost touch them. The glow of orange fires cast shadows over everyone.

Alex had that incredible guitar in his hands. He would play Flamenco music. She would feel the rhythms and the need to respond and she'd slip into sensual overload.

Rupert turned to see where her gaze was fixed. Leaning down so only she could hear, he said, "I think you fibbed, little Lara. I think you have a secret."

"No, I don't," she replied in a near whisper.

"That's too bad." Regret filled Rupert's tone, and her gaze rose to his face.

"I'm going to buy myself a cigar. Why don't you stay here and enjoy the concert."

"I'll go with you." She moved to follow him.

Shaking his head, he held her still. "Lara, Lara. You're not afraid to face down a toothless old lion, but you run from one with teeth. I expected more from you." Patting her hand, he left her standing in the plaza.

A lion with teeth. Alex. He could consume her, swallow her up with his music of life, and there would be no escape for her…none.

As Alex and Carlos took their seats, a crowd gathered.

She stood stock still behind the bodies, safely hidden from Alex's alert gaze. If she could just stay there, she would be protected from him and his voice.

Wrong.

The first chords rippled across the cold night air, La Guitarra crying out a mournful sound.

The music penetrated deep inside, to the place she kept hidden, safe from curious eyes. Every nerve in her body tingled.

She didn't want to listen, to feel, didn't want to see the images his music conjured. Visions of bubbling streams and battles filled her mind. Gypsy camps. Soldiers scooping women into their arms and galloping into the night.

Alex started to play his modern flamenco music.

Suddenly, a brilliant sunset filled Lara's mind, bringing light and warmth to every inch of her being. She wanted to sway and dip, to spin with pure delight.

What would it be like to be Lucia? To let go, to dance when she pleased, and how she pleased? She would close her eyes and let the music pour into her. It would flow out in vibrant dance. Lara's arms moved without conscious thought. She caught herself. Opening her eyes, she looked around. She'd been swaying, moving, almost dancing.

The people closest to her were watching her with curious sidelong glances.

Recovering quickly, Lara gave a small, embarrassed smile and hurried away from the plaza into the dark, twisting lanes of closed shops. She'd stay here until the performance was over, and then she could slip by everyone and make her way back to her car.

She wandered deeper into the shopping village, farther away from the noise of the concert, but distance didn't help. Reminders of Alex and his music were everywhere. She passed a shop with a painting easel in the window. It depicted a peasant village on the edge of the sea. Fishing nets were draped around and boats bobbed on the sparkling waters behind. A brilliant silver moon glowed over villagers gathered around a bonfire. All of them were dancing. Men and women, with their arms woven around each other, in and out of poses that seemed natural and normal, and yet so incredibly sensual.

Lara was certain if she looked close enough, she'd find the guitar player hidden in the picture, masterminding their movements.

"You wanted to dance. Why didn't you?"

The voice made her jump.

Alex had managed to finish the concert and escape the crowd to find her. It shouldn't have surprised her.

Turning slowly, she saw him standing inches away, dipped in shadows and silhouetted against the ebony sky behind him. A slice of moon lit one side of his features. His loose, white shirt fell in soft folds around his shoulders and over his hands. He looked like a troubadour out of the past...one who had come to sweep her off her feet. But Lara needed to keep herself firmly planted in the twenty-first century.

"I never dance in public," she said, her voice shaky.

"Ahh, yes, I forgot. You're not free to be yourself."

So close to the truth, his words pierced. How could he know her so well when no one else did? Even her own father didn't understand or guess at the turmoil inside her.

"I wasn't the performer tonight. You were." She shoved her hands in her coat pockets and stepped away from the shop window.

"But you were a part of my performance. I played for you."

Lara halted. She turned to look at him. His eyes were dark and sincere, his features open and vulnerable.

"Why? Why did you play for me?" she whispered.

He ran his fingers along her cheek. "Because when I look at you, I see my music. Everything I've ever felt, ever attempted to capture in lyrics and notes...I see it all in you, Lara. I think I've been writing for you all of my life."

She started to shake her head, but he captured her face with both his hands.

"Don't," he murmured as he touched his forehead to hers. "Don't deny what we both feel, Lara. I see the same thing in your eyes that's in my heart. No one feels the music as I do, not even Carlos. But you," he straightened so he could look at her. "When I play, there's a light in your eyes that can only come from a gypsy fire."

"We're not a fairy tale, Alex," she said. "We're not the guitar's lovers."

"Fairy tales are based on some truth. Some reality. Why not us? Do you have another explanation for this kinship? Have you ever felt this kind of attraction?"

She started to say she had kinship with Brett. But what did she really have with Brett? Their relationship was lost. Lara was lost. The only real thing in her life was the man holding her so tenderly and lighting sparks inside her. She wanted...needed to know what came after the sparks.

"No," she murmured, leaning towards him. "I've never felt like this."

He framed her face with his hands again. "If you believe nothing else, Lara, believe this. I've had a lot of relationships, some I'm not proud of, but this is different. This is real. Like my music. And I'm not going to let it go, Lara, not without a fight. Not without knowing..." He paused.

"Without knowing what?" Lara whispered, her lips inches away from his.

"Without knowing how you feel against me. Without knowing your heart belongs to me. Without knowing if this is as right as everything else about us."

His arms were around her, anchoring her to him. His lips parted slightly, as if he'd been waiting a long time to taste her and couldn't believe it was actually happening. He shifted, fitted her to him more closely and gently teased her mouth.

Lost in sensation, she opened her lips to him.

She'd never felt like this before. Never wanted more…never imagined that pure physical response could so completely take over. Not her. Not sensible, controlled Lara. But she was lost as Alex's hands slipped beneath her coat, pressing his warm fingers against her. He surrounded her, filled her with his warmth.

She caught her breath as hands stroked up over her back, along her waist. But she wanted more. She wanted her skin against his. Wanted to feel the warmth beneath his shirt. Whiskers rasped against her cheek, and she reveled in the contrasting sensations. Rough and smooth. Gentle hands with strength to break. A maelstrom of contradictions, wild and unpredictable, he made her feel as if she were flying through a storm…and she loved it.

Then, as if she stood right next to her, Lara heard Milly's voice, heard her prayer for protection and strength. Just like that, she snapped back to reality. Milly's prayers were answered. Lara pushed away from Alex. As she put distance between them, he frowned.

"What? Fraser, again?"

Lara shook her head. "No. It's all me, Alex. You said I needed to find myself and you were right. I'm trying. My faith is an important part of me and I won't betray it."

Surprise flitted over his features, and he stepped back.

"I'm sorry if you don't want to hear the truth."

"No…no. I'm actually very pleased to hear it, Lara. Surprised, but pleased. You really are discovering yourself. I can't help but be pleased." He didn't look pleased. He looked a little befuddled.

Lara didn't have time to question him as voices came from down the alley. A small group of people turned the corner.

"I knew he went this way."

Lara recognized Cynthia Halton's voice.

As an experienced fifteen-year-old in their Swiss boarding school, Cynthia had worked to perfect that breathy, sexy tone. "You slipped away so fast," she said to Alex. "We just had to find you and ask you some questions. Oh…we aren't interrupting anything, are we?"

Her blatantly calculated statement made Lara's skin crawl, and she couldn't find it in herself to respond.

"You're only interrupting if you intend to ask me personal questions I won't answer," Alex said in one smooth beat.

A startled silence followed his response.

Alex put Cynthia on the defensive.

One of the men in the group chuckled. "No more personal than asking where I can find your music. I'm very impressed with your technique," the young man said. "I'm a fan of Flamenco—traditional, of course. I've never been very interested in the modern performers…until yesterday when you performed."

Alex thanked him and they talked about guitars, styles, and performers Lara had never heard of. A slight breeze shimmied up her coat and brushed over her sensitized skin. She shivered.

"Are you cold, Lara?" Alex turned his attention back to her. "Would you like me to walk you back to the fire?"

She shook her head abruptly, imagining what Cynthia would make of it. "Thanks, but don't interrupt your conversation. I think I'll be leaving, anyway." After saying goodnight, she eased away from the group.

Alex's rigid stance told her he was not pleased, but he said nothing.

As she reached the corner, Cynthia said, "Say hello to Brett for me."

Lara gritted her teeth and strode toward the entrance of Tlaquepaque Village, but somehow became confused. She turned down alley after alley, each one more dark than the previous. She was a little frightened by the time she rounded yet another corner and heard voices somewhere in the dark.

"Are you threatening me?" Troy's unmistakable voice rose above the others.

9

Startled, Lara edged to the corner and peeked around. At the end of the lane, Troy stood facing two large men. Both of them were muscular and bulky, like body builders. Light reflected off one of the men's faces, and his features struck a familiar chord.

He said something to Troy that Lara couldn't hear.

Troy's reaction was plain. His body straightened and his face set in hard, rigid lines. "You are out of your minds. I've already told your boss, I will have nothing to do with this. We have a legal business transaction between us which will be fulfilled, but what you're asking now, I won't even consider." He practically spat out the words. Then, spinning on one heel, he turned and disappeared from sight.

The men spoke in low tones for a few moments, and then left the alley in the opposite direction.

Lara released a breath. What did these men want Troy to do? And who was their boss? The way he'd said the word, he obviously had no respect for whoever it was. Was their boss the person Troy had met in the woods earlier today? Lara was sure of it. The person had obviously delivered a message and these men had shown up tonight for an answer. But who was the mysterious boss? What legal transaction did Troy have with the man? Did he want Troy to do something illegal? Is that why Troy refused to do it?

Lara had known Troy all of her life. He was a man

of deep conviction. He followed the letter of the law. She didn't think he'd ever even had a parking ticket. So why did these thugs—and that's what they were, thugs—think they could sway him? What made them think they could convince him to do something illegal?

Eliza had said Troy was deep in debt, so deep in fact, Eliza was afraid. Could Troy have borrowed money from these men? Was the legal business transaction he mentioned a loan? Did they think they could use his debts to force him to do something illegal?

What in the world did they want him to do?

Her mind whirled with possibilities. Then she remembered the missing checks in Brett's ledger and suddenly, all her whirling, spinning thoughts settled in the pit of her stomach.

Were these men pressuring Troy to take money from Fallon Enterprises to cover his debts? It seemed plausible. He had the means. With his office right next to Brett's, Troy was in and out every day.

No one, not even Brett, would question Troy if he lingered over Brett's desk...just long enough to remove the checks. It seemed plausible, even possible. But Troy had resisted the pressure. He'd just told those men in no uncertain terms he would not do as they asked. So, who had taken the checks?

Lara covered her face with her hands. It was too much to comprehend, too difficult not to trust her friends and family. She felt as if she were drowning. Spinning, she headed back the way she had come, and soon found her way to her car, managing to avoid the crowd in the plaza. Sliding into the back seat, she huddled into the corner.

The driver stopped in front of the guesthouse.

Lights in the living room indicated Brett was home, probably waiting to talk to her.

Lara flopped back against the seat, wishing she could tell the driver to get back on the road and drive. She didn't have the strength to face Brett tonight. But she didn't act quickly enough and the driver opened her car door. She stepped out, thanked him, buttoned her jacket, and then stood just outside the door, hesitating.

The driver waited. He wouldn't leave until she went inside.

Sighing, she trudged up the sidewalk and inside.

Brett stood across the room, facing the patio doors. The small balcony looked down the canyon toward town and offered an angled view of the town's lights. One hand in his pocket, Brett stared out at the lights, cradling a bottle of water in his other hand. "Hello," he said in a subdued voice.

"Hi."

He gestured to the phone with the glass. "Your father's been trying to talk to me all day so I decided to come back here and wait for his call."

She nodded, pulling her coat tighter, even though it was buttoned.

"I thought it might be a good time for us to clear the air."

She nodded again, wishing she could just slip into her room. But she didn't trust her voice.

Brett must have felt the same way because the silence stretched on. He sighed once and turned back toward the city lights. "Do you know what my major was in school, Lara?"

Puzzled, she said, "Business. My father only recruits business majors."

"Yes, but I had a specialty. My thesis was on non-profit organizations and fundraising for charities. At twenty-two, I knew more about sponsorship for non-profits than many men twice my age."

Lara was stunned. Her father had no need for someone with those unique skills. "So why did my father recruit you? I remember he was determined to hire you."

Brett shrugged. "I was bright, created a lot of waves in college and he liked my integrity. He believed that was one of my best attributes."

It all made sense, but Brett had had little opportunity to use his skills until now.

"But then…" she started to say.

Brett interrupted her. "But then I should have been the perfect choice to open your mother's school. I should have seen the pitfalls, anticipated the objections, seen to it there were enough sponsorships. I know, Lara. Believe me, I know. It's very apparent how badly I've failed." He took a long sip of water.

Lara stood silent.

The water bottle crackled as he turned to the window. "I don't know what happened. Nothing has been right since I got here. Maybe even for a long time before I left New York. I can't seem to see my way clear. I'm not sure I even know what's right and wrong anymore." His tone was forlorn.

Lara ached. "Brett," she hesitated. He turned to face her and the pain on his handsome face caused a new wash of pity. "What's causing your confusion?" she asked. "You've always been the most focused, dedicated person I know."

"Yes, I have. But what have I been dedicated to? Climbing your father's corporate latter and currying his favor? Do you know what an impossible task that is? It's hard to even meet his expectations, let alone please him. I never quite knew where I stood."

Lara was silent. A chill began to replace the guilt inside her. Was Alex right about Brett? Had he used her to gain favor with her father? Had ambition been the driving force in his life? Any minute he was going to make an admission she didn't want to hear.

"You, on the other hand, were easy to read," he said, turning to meet her gaze. A slight smile played over his lips. "When I walked into a room, your face lit up. You looked at me as if I were the best thing to ever happen to you. No matter how many mistakes I made or how small I looked in your father's eyes, you made me feel like something special every time I was with you."

Lara struggled to understand.

In the silence he said, "You don't look at me like that anymore."

The weight in her stomach dropped again, deeper and deeper as he stared at her across the space, his expression wounded and hurt. She hadn't expected him to say this...and she wished he hadn't. Guilt washed over her in tidal waves.

This man had stood by her side through the worst possible trauma.

"You were terribly young and very vulnerable," he continued. "You needed a friend so badly, Lara. I was only too glad to step in and fill the role of knight in shining armor. I desperately needed the ego boost after dealing with my not-so-spectacular entry into the corporate world. But now you're healthier, better, a little wiser, and I've become a tarnished knight."

"Brett," she murmured. "You're not a tarnished

knight. What you did was wonderful. Admirable. I shouldn't have allowed your kindness to turn into a trap."

He turned a startled gaze on her.

"If I've made you feel tarnished, Brett, then I owe you much more than apology. You were my friend. A good friend. Let's just leave it there."

"No, Lara. I have to say this. If I were really a good friend, I would never have let you think this was something more. But I let our relationship develop too far, too fast. You wanted it, so I wanted to make it happen. It's the story of my life. I've tried to keep everyone happy instead of following my instincts. As a result, I've let the school's finances get out of hand. All of this is happening because I'm not the man I once was." His words were stricken. The pain in his tone and his brutal honesty were raw and aching.

Had he taken the checks from his own ledger? But what would be the purpose...unless he was trying to cover his actions.

She stumbled through her words. "Brett, how can I help?"

He shook his head. "You can't. If I let you dig me out of this then I'll never be able to get back to where I need to be. I won't respect myself and no one else will, either."

Slowly, she nodded. "I understand." Still she had questions.

Was he taking responsibility for more than their relationship, perhaps for the problems surrounding the school? If they were friends, why couldn't he confide in her? Did he still think of her as child, a helpless invalid? Or maybe someone he could control.

Her blood ran cold.

"Thanks. I knew I could count on you." His tone of voice made her feel predictable, an easily controlled and manipulated child.

The phone rang.

"That's your father. This is probably going to be a long call." Brett moved to answer.

Lara waited, hoping he would tell her father everything.

But he was all business and updates. Apparently, he didn't plan to confess his misuse of funds tonight.

Spinning, Lara headed for her room. She scrubbed her face, slid into a nightgown and climbed into bed, exhausted. The day had been a roller coaster ride of emotion. She tossed and turned.

Had Brett's whole conversation tonight been orchestrated to make her feel sorry for him so he could guilt her into silence? It was an unpleasant possibility.

She'd known Brett for five years, and found it hard to believe he would steal from her father.

But people changed.

No one who knew Lara would have believed she would confront her father's friends and face down Rupert Townsend.

She wanted...needed a sounding board, someone to talk to. Brett *was* that person, but she couldn't talk to him about Troy's strange behavior or tell him she didn't trust him. So whom could she talk to?

A dark-haired man with a velvet voice strolled through her mind. She believed she could trust Alex. But Lara didn't know if she could trust *herself* with Alex.

The bed suddenly seemed too confining. She flung back the covers and strode to the window. Tugging the chord, she opened the shades, allowing silvery moonlight to spill into the room. The bright crescent peeked over the mountain, filling the canyon with gentle light. Behind it, stars glowed. The trees were silent, strong, and ever present.

Lara eased down, clasped her hands, focused on the peaceful land outside, and prayed.

~*~

When Lara arrived at the main house the next morning, Christy was waiting, a big smile pasted on her face. The girl threw her arms around Lara.

"What was that for?" Lara laughed as she rocked back on her heels.

"I'm glad to see you. I wasn't sure you would come this morning."

"Why?"

"Mom's taking all of the visitors down to Jerome for a tour. It's an Old West town turned into kind of an artist's colony. She said you would like it and I shouldn't be disappointed if you didn't come today."

"She's right. I would like it." Lara cupped Christy's chin and tilted her face up. "But you and I have a deal, and I don't disappoint my friends."

Christy's hug nearly broke her in two. "I can't wait to do this. Let's get started."

"Aren't you sore today?"

"A little. But nothing like I thought I would be. I feel great…like my body's glad to be moving. I'm ready to go, and I can't wait to hear Alex's song again."

Lara hesitated as she pulled the floor mats out of her bag. She hoped Alex had made the trip to Jerome. After more sensual, gypsy-fire dreams, she didn't feel confident about her ability to keep her resolution. Alex was a temptation she didn't need. All she wanted was to stretch her body and lose herself in the slow, controlled dance movements.

Silently, she laid out the mats, popped a CD in the player and launched into her workout routine.

Christy followed along. When they came to an exercise she didn't remember she mimicked Lara's moves. Halfway through their routine, Christy's smile had faded and turned into a frowning look of concentration.

Alex breezed into the room.

Lara's heart jumped and sank at the same time. She should have known keeping her course would not be easy.

"Good morning, ladies." His smile was for Christy. He barely even glanced at Lara. Crossing the room in strong, purposeful strides, he took his chair from the corner and sat at the window. "Don't let me interrupt your workout," he said, as he tuned his guitar. Without another word, he launched into a run of ascending and descending chords, each more difficult than the first. He didn't play the repetitive song he'd worked on the day before until some time had passed.

Her student flashed Lara a secretive smile. Christy was imbued with a new enthusiasm. They worked until sweat beaded on both their faces and fatigue sat like a live thing on Christy's small frame.

"I think maybe we overdid it," Lara said in a subdued voice.

Christy shook her head. "I'll be fine after I relax in the spa. You are coming today, aren't you?"

Lara glanced back at Alex. "I..." The look on Christy's face broke Lara's resolve. "I said I would, didn't I?"

"Great. Let's go. I think I need it." Turning to the man in the corner, Christy raised her voice. "Excuse me, Alex. I'm sorry to interrupt your song, but we're heading down to the spa. Wanna come with us?"

Lara held her breath.

"I need to work a little longer. Maybe I'll join you after a while."

Relief swept through Lara and she rolled her mat quickly, hoping to make an escape.

"Don't forget, OK?" Christy smiled at Alex, and crossed to the door, where she turned to Lara. "You won't be long, will you? Ten minutes?"

"Ten."

Christy looked back at Alex. "It won't be half as much fun without you. Please say you'll come."

"I'm sure you two can have much more fun without me. You can talk about things without me around."

"No, we won't. We're a threesome. We want you to come," Christy replied.

Alex plucked at his guitar, purposely looking away. "Maybe Lara would feel better if I were not there."

Christy turned to Lara, her expression questioning.

Lara remembered her dream, how imaginary Luisa felt beautiful and perfect. Lara could not boast of any perfection. Her legs were scarred and damaged. She didn't want Alex to see.

Then again, he would see all her imperfections and be turned off. This mystical, midnight attraction would die in the face of reality. Maybe it was just the solution she needed.

"I'd like you to come with us," she said, now anxious for the opportunity.

He searched her face for the truth. After a moment, he rose from his seat at the window. "I'll join you shortly."

Lara hurried to the guesthouse, wondering if she'd done the right thing. When she opened the door, the phone was ringing. She hurried to pick it up.

Her father was on the other end. They talked for a long while, but after a time, his questions became pointed. He probed, searching for answers. How was Brett? Did she find him different? What was he doing? How was the event going?

"It'd be going much better if you were here." She spoke without thinking.

A sudden, dead silence at the other end indicated her father wasn't pleased. "Are you saying Brett is mishandling things?"

So, he suspected something was not right. Why didn't he come right out and ask Brett? Her father's actions irritated her.

"No, that's not it at all. I'm saying all of this would have been much easier on everyone if you'd been here. This is Mother's project. Brett and Troy are trying their best to make it happen, but it's been difficult. I think it deserved more of your attention."

This time the silence at the other end sizzled. After a few moments he said, "Well, it's apparent something has happened."

"If it's so apparent, why aren't you here?"

"You sound like a child, Lara, whining for attention."

Resentment flared. "You're making me feel like one, Dad. And besides, I deserve more attention. This project deserves attention! Do you know how many incredibly talented children are out there and how much help they need?"

"When did you decide to become my social conscience?" It was meant to be sarcastic, to jolt her back into her place. All it really did was infuriate her.

"When you decided to stop listening to yours."

"I made a difficult business decision. Next time, I'll be sure to consult you," he snapped back.

"Please, Dad," sarcasm dripped from her tone. "This wasn't about business. This was about Mom. This was her dream and you couldn't even spare a week to make it work." She didn't need to see him to know how much she'd hurt him. The silence stretched. Lara wondered how she'd managed to be so cruel.

When her father finally spoke, she heard cold control in his voice. "If I'd known this was going to be my reception, I wouldn't have wasted my time or money calling all the way from London."

Anger flamed to life again, effectively burning away any residue of guilt. "I'm sorry for your wasted effort, too. Next time I'll let Brett pick up the phone and you'll get all the 'yes sirs' you were obviously looking for. Good-bye, Dad." She hung up and stalked toward her bedroom. Tossing her dance bag to the corner, she threw herself on the bed.

Exactly what had just happened? She couldn't remember the last time she'd had an argument with her father. Certainly, it was before the accident in her slightly rebellious teen years. Since then, they'd always managed to discuss issues and to talk things out. So how did this conversation go so wrong?

Did her father manipulate her and Brett against one another to find out what he needed to know, to keep them both in line?

Her father really had pushed them together. He had always been concerned that she would be a target for fortune hunters. But he liked and trusted Brett. An attachment between the two of them certainly lessened her father's concerns.

The realization made her angry.

How simple it had been for him to put two needy, nubile young people together and let nature take its course. Rather than letting Lara step out into the shark-infested waters of the real world, his way was less risky.

Alex was right.

She'd been controlled to make her parents' lives easy. The revelation stung.

Her father, not wanting to face the loss of his wife, had invested little emotion into the school and sent Brett to take his place.

Lara's hurt was sharp and poignant, like it had been in the days after her mother's death. Tears burned and she fell back, burying her face in the pillows. Grief was an old enemy, but she refused to succumb to its emptiness this time. She rolled to her side and glimpsed the clock. Thirty minutes had passed.

Alex and Christy were waiting for her in the spa.

Jumping out of bed, she pulled on a swimsuit and wrapped a dance skirt around her. Grabbing a towel from the bathroom, she headed for the spa.

Christy was laughing at something Alex said, her back to the walkway. Alex looked up when he saw Lara.

Christy turned. "We thought you chickened out," she said, laughter still in her voice.

"I didn't. I had a call from my father in London.

Besides, what's there to be afraid of?"

"Hop in," Christy said, laughing and scooting to the other side of the octagon-shaped spa.

Lara hesitated. Loosening the strings of her multicolored wrap-around skirt was challenging. She walked to a nearby patio table and placed her towel on it. "You were right, Christy," she said, stalling. "This spa is perfectly situated."

The edge of the patio marked the boundaries of the property. The pool filled the space. She could see down the canyon all the way to the valley. Even in the daylight, the view was lovely. At night, with the town lights sparkling, it would be spectacular.

Christy chatted about how she spent long hours in the spa, even on the coldest days.

Lara barely heard. Her disappointment in her father was a raw, aching wound. If she stood now, and removed her skirt, Alex's rejection would add to her pain. She didn't think she could bear it.

Her father was hiding, refusing to face his fears, and letting the people he cared about face the consequences...and she was acting just like him. It was a comparison she couldn't bear. She untied her skirt and tugged it free.

Alex watched her.

She walked straight to the edge of the spa. Staunchly, she placed one foot in the warm water. Her legs were level with Alex's head, inches from his gaze. Her scars were in full view from thigh to shin.

His gaze was on her, sweeping up her body as she went down the steps, one at a time.

When the water reached her waist, she eased onto the seat.

Heat filled Alex's gaze. His desire sizzled from

across the spa. Christy said something and he looked away, masking the smoldering flames.

Lara leaned back, letting the jets and bubbles sweep over her body in a rush of pleasure. She felt beautiful. Alex had seen the scars and was still attracted to her. Resting her head on the edge of the spa, Lara looked up at the bright blue sky and laughed out loud.

"What's so funny?" Christy asked.

"This feels wonderful."

"Told you this was a great idea," Christy said.

Alex's soft, knowing smile made Lara laugh again.

Christy was full of energy and talked continuously, covering every topic from her favorite song to her parents' fights.

Lara was amazed at how patient Alex was with her.

He teased and even challenged her to be more understanding with her parents. "It's hard to make a marriage work. How many other parents do you know who are still together?"

The cloudless sky was a perfect blue, the water warm and soothing.

Christy's giggles were infectious.

Alex's strong voice warmed and reassured Lara. Patience and compassion filled his tone as he spoke to this troubled little girl...and Lara fell a little more in love with him.

He could hold an audience captive in his hand and play them like an instrument. He could reach inside someone to find the hidden person. He brought moments of beauty to his music and shared them.

Lara loved his fearlessness and his strength of will. As he leaned his arms against the back of the spa, she found it difficult to keep from gliding across the water, and kissing him until he knew how he made her feel. Thoughts of what Christy might think stopped her. Jerking to her feet, Lara stepped out. The sudden cold rasped against her sensitive skin, and she shivered.

Alex laughed, which only made her shiver more.

"I think she's trying to tell us something," Alex said to Christy.

"I guess it is time to get out. I just don't want it to end yet," Christy said.

"Then let's not let it end. Let's do something else."

"Like what?"

"How about lunch in town and a jeep tour of the canyon?"

Christy turned to Lara. "What do you think?"

"I promised Brett I'd do some work at the school this afternoon."

"We'll take a short tour and you can go to the school afterwards." Alex suggested.

There were carefully banked flames in Alex's gaze, a knowing tilt of the lips she was dying to kiss, and Lara knew she was playing with fire.

"The school. Always the school. It seems like my whole life is about the school." Christy's statement was a perfectly prepared guilt trip. And it worked.

Fire or not, Christy deserved some attention.

"All right. You win," Lara said. "But it will have to be a short tour."

Something flashed in Alex's eyes.

Lara had the feeling she'd leapt straight into the flames.

10

Christy slurped the last of her chocolate malt, and then giggled. "Sorry." She grinned over the tall glass. "It just tasted too good."

"I should have ordered one." Lara couldn't help smiling.

"See, I told you this was the day to let go and have fun. You'll probably be hungry before we get back from our tour."

"If we get a tour. I had no idea you needed reservations this time of year."

Lara and Christy sat at the restaurant's patio table finishing their lunch.

Alex was searching for a tour to take them through the nearby canyons. The possibility didn't look promising.

"Even if we don't get to go, this morning has been great," Christy said.

"Yes, it has."

Christy frowned as another thought came to her. "Saturday is coming up fast. It'll be the last day of the opening ceremonies."

"You sound like you don't want this week to end."

Christy shrugged. "I miss my mom and dad. It'll be nice to have time with them again, but everyone else will be leaving. Alex will, and maybe you. It'll be so boring."

"We'll find a good stable and a horse you like and

you'll be able to ride every day. That'll be something to look forward to."

Something sparked in Christy's eyes. "Maybe if I stay healthy, my parents will let me have a horse."

Maybe a horse *was* the right solution for Christy. Lara decided to speak to Eliza about it.

Alex returned with tickets fanned out in his hand.

Christy's face lit with a wide grin. "I knew you'd get them!" she exclaimed.

It's the last tour of the day, and they're waiting for us now." He gestured across the street to a line of outlandishly painted jeeps...all pink.

"Cool!" Christy rose slowly from her chair. The stilted movement was a visual opposite to her enthusiastic response.

"Are you sure you're up to this?" Lara asked.

"I'm not going to miss it. If I have to, I'll go spend another two hours in the spa."

Lara grabbed her backpack and followed Christy across the street. Alex held out his hand. She took it and he pulled her across the street, ahead of the oncoming traffic. Alex introduced their driver, Kurt, a twenty-ish, sun-bleached blond who looked and sounded as if he'd just stepped off a California beach. Smiling, Kurt led the way and they piled into their vehicle. Lara and Christy settled in the back.

Looking up at the bright blue sky, broken only by a few wisps of white clouds, Lara laughed out loud.

Christy giggled, too.

"Hey, no laughing without me." Alex looked over his shoulder.

Christy and Lara looked at each other and giggled again.

The driver turned the jeep down a back street and

climbed the mountains behind Sedona.

As they picked up speed, the wind sliced through Lara's hair. She tugged two hairbands and baseball caps out of her backpack and handed a set to Christy. They tied their hair back and tucked the ponytails through the caps. Lara pulled sunscreen out, too. "We're both going to need this."

Without argument, red-haired, freckle-faced Christy squeezed the sunscreen into her hands and rubbed it over her face and arms.

~*~

Kurt talked about the vegetation, the desert, the animals, and the geology that had formed the impressive red rocks. They followed the dirt road deeper into the mountains, and he told them about Sedona's history, how the Indians considered the canyon sacred.

Alex listened, but all the while, his mind was on other things...the criminals who traveled from around the world to loot the burial grounds of ancient people. How could he help put a stop to it? And how involved was Lara in her father's corporation?

The little utility vehicle climbed through Bear Wallow Canyon until they were fifteen hundred feet above Sedona. The pine trees and dark green vegetation grew denser. They came around a corner of the trail and the mountain disappeared, leaving the vast plain spread out below. Kurt stopped just off the trail.

They climbed out and crossed to a rocky outcropping.

Golden sandstone ridges looked as if streams had

cut them just yesterday. Massive red rock outcroppings stood like sentinels. Below, a belt of lush green spread across the red dirt like a blanket with perfect edges. And of course, the sky was the cobalt blue Alex had come to expect from Sedona.

"All I want to do is sit and drink it in." Lara drew a deep breath.

Camera in hand, Christy moved over the rock, searching for the best angle.

"That outcropping gives the most unobstructed view." Kurt pointed to another ledge of boulders about ten yards below.

"I want to go down there."

"I'll walk you down," Kurt offered. They started out. Kurt held Christy's arm as she moved slowly, carefully placing her feet on the steep trail. All the way, Kurt gestured with his other hand to the trees and the view, talking while Christy listened raptly.

"He's very good with her," Lara said, watching them walk down. "Did you talk to him about her illness?"

Alex shook his head. "I didn't need to. He's observant, and he does his job well."

The two below reached the outcropping and Christy stood on the edge, snapping pictures.

"This is all too amazing. I can't believe how far she's come in just two days," Lara said.

"Christy was suffering from depression. It's as debilitating as any physical ailment."

"A little helping hand brought her out of it. It was so easy. I wonder what other kids would accomplish if given half a chance?"

"What kids?"

"I was going through the applications for the

school and found kids with wonderful talents. They also had devastating disabilities, and no income to afford the tuition. They were looking for scholarships and grants...which we don't offer. But I can't stop thinking about them."

Alex strove for a casual tone. "I didn't realize you had invested so much time and work into your mother's school."

"I didn't. I just found out about them."

"So why weren't plans made for those children?" Alex hated delving in too deep.

"Budget cuts."

Alex had the distinct feeling there was more. "Budget cuts in Fallon Enterprises?"

"The school isn't really a Fallon project. If it was, we might be in a better position."

"I don't understand. Why isn't your father involved?"

"He handed this project over to Troy and Brett two years ago. I'm not even sure he signs the checks."

Alarm bells rang in Alex's head. "That's a lot of money to just sign away."

Lara laughed but it wasn't a happy sound. "I'm sure my father is aware. He's willing to spend a lot of money in my mother's name, but not to be involved."

"That doesn't make any sense."

Her expression was so sad it made him ache. "It does if being here is too painful for him. Sedona was my mother's favorite place in the world. She would have lived here full time if my father's business had not forced him to stay in New York. The first thing he did after my mother died was to sell our house here. He hasn't been back since."

"I see." An absentee, disinterested owner would

make deception possible, even easy. The entire Fallon School of Art could be a base of operations for the shipping of illegally obtained Chaco pottery without Daniel Fallon even knowing. With so little focused on school curriculum, Alex thought that might be the case. "What's being done about the problems I mentioned?"

Lara shook her head and made a little sound of frustration. "Nothing. Absolutely nothing."

Were her friends involved in a covert operation and not the business of running the school?

"Don't they realize they're losing investors and all this week's efforts will fail?"

"I think both Troy and Brett are overwhelmed. Brett's dealing with some...financial issues and Troy's wrapped up in personal problems. They're doing their best just to keep their heads above water. Besides, my mother's background was education. Curriculum was her arena. I don't think either of them really even knew where to begin."

"Maybe I can help." This was the opportunity he'd been waiting for. Why was he hesitating?

Maybe because the next step would signal the beginning of the end. Nothing would be the same between Lara and him after this.

Feeling like he was hammering nails into his coffin he said, "I'll set up an appointment to talk to Troy and Fraser."

~*~

As the utility vehicle snaked its way down the mountain, Lara mulled over Alex's offer. Christy and Kurt's return had prevented any discussion, but it was an exciting prospect. Before the accident curtailed her university attendance, Lara had wanted to focus on education like her mother.

During the long months of inactivity, she'd taken some online courses to finish her degree. Now the idea of working with Alex on a program for children with special needs lit a banked fire.

Ideas flowed. She hardly noticed the beautiful scenery passing by, until they rounded a corner to a downhill stretch perched on the side of a slope. The valley lay far below in another spectacular view. Lara focused on it, letting its beauty fill her.

"What's this guy doing?" Kurt muttered the words as if he hadn't intended to let them out.

Everyone turned to look behind them.

Lara gasped as a huge black SUV barreled toward them.

Kurt slowed their jeep, attempting to move to the left, closer to the hillside, but the SUV gunned the motor and cut them off. Kurt swerved to avoid hitting the other vehicle, swinging outward.

Christy screamed, and Lara grabbed her.

Kurt quickly adjusted the vehicle to a straight path but they were perilously close to the edge.

The SUV moved up, parallel with Lara. Arms wrapped around Christy, Lara looked over her shoulder. The windows were tinted so dark she could barely make out the people, though their silhouettes were clear. She recognized the baldhead of one and the distinctive, longish, slicked-back hair of the other. The sight chilled her to the bone. The driver and the man in the passenger's seat were the two men she'd seen in the alley last night with Troy.

The driver gunned the engine and the SUV shot ahead of them, its big tires leaving a trail of dust behind.

Kurt pulled into the center of the road and stopped. "Well, I guess they were in a real big hurry." He smiled as he turned to the back seat. "Everyone all right?" His smile was for Christy.

Lara had a death hold on the young girl. Releasing her, Lara looked around. "Yes," she lied. "We're fine." She wasn't sure she'd ever be fine again.

Christy grinned. "Wow. One adventure after another. This has been an awesome day!"

Lara smiled, too, but she didn't dare look at Alex for fear he'd see the lie in her eyes. She was silent for the rest of the way home, her mind turning over and over the vision of the driver and his passenger.

The two mysterious strangers had endangered Christy…Lara closed her eyes and swallowed hard.

Kurt joked around and took Christy's mind off the event. Alex helped. Between the two of them, they had her laughing and talking about the much-anticipated horseback-riding trip.

Those men had followed them…had followed Troy's daughter, and almost pushed the car she was riding in over a cliff. Was it the next-level threat? If Troy didn't do what they wanted him to do, would they hurt Christy?

Horror washed over Lara in waves.

What did they want him to do? What could be so important they'd be willing to harm a little girl?

Money. It had to be about money. Troy could sell some of his antiquities, and he would have money. But they must have wanted him to do something illegal…something that would give them more than Troy could.

Fallon Enterprises' assets were phenomenal. Troy

had access to the company. And Brett was covering for him. It would explain a lot.

If Brett had made the mistakes he talked about, he was smart enough to own up to them with her father and stop the situation before it escalated. But if Brett was covering for someone else, someone who wasn't as sensible about money...this scenario would explain Brett's behavior perfectly. He wouldn't lie to protect himself, but he would definitely protect the people he cared about.

Brett couldn't put high amounts on those checks. Three missing checks would barely tap into the company's funds and would only cause red flags to go up in the finance department. Then Brett would be on the hot seat, and the game would be over.

Unless, of course, the checks were only the first in a series. Maybe those men intended to blackmail Troy and Brett to give money in small amounts until a fortune had been drained from Fallon Enterprises.

Possible, but that would require massive planning. Why would someone go to all the trouble to set up a blackmail scheme for small deposits of money that could be easily discovered and stopped? There had to be something else those men were after.

Lara rubbed her forehead as the vehicle pulled to a stop in front of the tour company's main office. Thankful for the distraction, she climbed out of the vehicle as Christy hugged Kurt and thanked him for the trip.

"Kurt, your calm expertise was invaluable." Alex turned to Lara. "Why don't you and Christy go on ahead to the car? I'll be right there." He pulled some bills out of his wallet.

Christy started to chatter about the trip.

Alex said something about the license plate to Kurt. Good. Alex had caught the number.

Christy sat between Lara and Alex. Lara studiously avoided making eye contact with Alex. Using Christy as a buffer, she adroitly focused on the young girl's excited talk as they wound their way home. At the house, Christy skipped ahead, anxious to tell her mother everything, but Eliza was running errands.

Alex took Lara's arm.

She turned to look into a dark, cold expression.

"Do you mind telling me what's going on?"

Lara shifted. "What do you mean?"

"What has you so scared you turned white as a sheet and can barely talk now?"

"I'm not a child like Christy, Alex. I know the real danger we were in. Of course I'm upset."

"Don't give me that. You saw those men and froze up like a blocked steam engine. What's going on?"

Maybe he could help her with this. But if she explained she'd be revealing Troy's secret and Brett's problems. They were not hers to reveal.

Christy called her name.

"I have to go to Christy." She left him standing tight-lipped in the entryway.

Christy's nurse took the girl firmly in hand and dictated another hour in the spa for the overused muscles and wired senses. Christy chatted endlessly about the trip, the view, and the near mishap. She would tell her father and mother.

Troy might put two and two together after such a close call. If Troy knew they had threatened Christy, what choice would he have but to do as they asked?

Lara rubbed her forehead again. She needed more

time to think things through, to find a way to help Troy. She made her escape and hurried across the grounds to avoid Alex. She needed to find her way through one dilemma before she tackled another. Alex Summers was a problem too daunting to face. She slipped inside the guesthouse and locked the door.

The answering machine light blinked. Hurrying across the room, she punched the button. Brett's voice filled the air.

"Hi, Lara. I tried your cell phone but you didn't answer. Please call me as soon as you get this. Troy and I are on our way to Flagstaff to pick up the donor plaques. We gave the school workers the rest of the day off before I remembered I've got a new batch of applications coming in today. Could you swing by the school and look them over, I'd be very thankful. Use the same criteria to sort through them as you did before. Give me a buzz when you get this. Thanks."

The same criteria. More children to be turned away. Lara didn't know if she could stand to go through another batch. But it gave her the excuse she needed. She messaged Brett then headed to the garage to find a driver.

Using her code, Lara stepped into the silent school. She went straight to Brett's office and retrieved the applications. Going through them required little time, since the only criteria was the ability to pay the tuition. She flagged the appropriate files, and then began her real work.

On top of the desk was a folder with receipts inside. Only the most recent were listed, but after doing a quick summary, Lara was astonished by the figure. Ten thousand dollars in receipts and preparations in the last few days. Money seemed to be slipping through Brett's fingers like water. No wonder he was worried.

She searched the rest of the desk but found nothing out of the ordinary—except the check ledger no longer sat on his desk. Lara pushed the mouse, the computer screen popped up. She searched the files on the desktop, but she had no passwords to access bookkeeping accounts and was not willing to invade Brett's privacy. There was a file with her mother's name. Lara had no qualms about accessing it, since it was not locked. The file contained notes, memorandums, and letters her mother had written about the school. The curriculum had obviously been on her mind. She'd already contacted a leading teaching university in the Midwest and had scheduled meetings with several professors from a university. Her mother had planned a curriculum but the accident ended all her plans.

Why, Lord? Why did you take her? She could have done so much good. Reached so many children. Why did you leave me and take her?

Everything was falling apart. The school's future. Her friends' lives. Things would be right if her mother were still alive. Rising from the desk, she walked to the window.

Brett's office was at the back of the school. Directly in front of her was the ragged crag Alex had climbed. She looked at the top, wishing she could be there. If she could just climb high enough, surely she could find the answers she needed. She fixed her gaze on the top, filled with a yearning she hadn't experienced since she was a child. At the back of her mind, she heard Alex's voice, urging her to move forward, to fly.

Why not?

The face of the crag was solid rock, too sheer and too dangerous for her to scale, but if she moved slightly west where the ascent was less steep...she glanced at her watch. Three forty. Two hours before dusk. Plenty of time. She opened the back door, strode across the gravel yard, and hopped the low retaining wall. In moments, she stood at the base of the crag.

Up close it seemed larger, steeper.

But Lara was determined. She climbed, angling toward the right, away from the rocky bluff. The ground was hard and solid. Soon she hit gravel and small rocks, lost her footing and slid downhill. She scraped her palms and banged her shins several times, but she kept going.

She was not even close to the top. Taking the fire road to the top would be easier and faster. Continuing to the right would be an easy ascent, too. But the challenge was to the left. Lara made an abrupt turn, veering toward the bluff. She climbed until her legs ached, and she was out of breath. All her daily workouts had not prepared her for altitude challenges. Her legs began to feel a little shaky so she slowed, giving them the opportunity to rest.

She'd probably been climbing for forty-five minutes. Ahead, a massive rock completely filled her vision. She couldn't see around or above it. The ground beneath was steep and slippery. If she took that way, she ran the risk of sliding twenty feet back down the hill.

Her only choice was to go over it. She dug her tennis shoes into the soil and searched for hand holds. Pulling and crawling up the rounded rock was easy enough, but this rock was just the first in an outcropping.

She could go around, but Lara didn't want the easy way out. The first few feet were easy. Her legs were steady. She stepped into a foothold. As she put all of her weight on it, solid ground crumbled. Lara slid down the rocky face, hands scraping and fingers digging into the rock.

Her foot hit a ledge, and she jolted to a sliding stop. Pain shot up her leg. She froze, perched on one leg, barely daring to breathe. She took several calming breaths, suddenly remembering why Troy had never climbed this crag.

He said Eliza needed him.

Fear washed through Lara. She searched for something else to grab, somewhere to put her foot so she could climb up. But she'd slid over a sheer stretch and managed to catch the only foothold. There was nowhere to go, up or down. She stayed frozen, one foot poised on a narrow foothold, the other pressed against the slick rock. Her legs shook. She was afraid to move...even to look up or down. Terrified, she flattened against the rock and closed her eyes.

11

"Look to your left, Lara. Lean into the leg that's steady and reach for the corner." Alex's voice calmed and reassured her.

The rocky outcropping was only a foot away. How had she missed it?

Leaning forward, her fingers gripped the rock and she pulled herself around the corner. With her free leg, she stepped on the broken rocks and moved clear of the sheer face.

Alex had only been five feet below. It seemed he understood her need to do it on her own. Lara dragged her tongue over dry lips.

"Aren't you going to tell me how foolish this was?"

"Was it foolish?"

"Probably. But it's my neck to risk, isn't it?"

He gestured to the sheer rock face. "Eventually you would have calmed down and seen the way out or you would have slid down, earning yourself more scrapes and bruises, but I doubt you would have done any serious damage. I don't think it was much of a risk."

"I suppose you take much greater risks?"

"I don't have an army of concerned friends and family telling me what to do."

"Did you come all the way up here just to bait me?"

"I thought I came to save you," he said.

"According to you, I wasn't in danger and didn't need saving, so you won't be getting any thanks. What are you doing here?"

"Following you. What else have I done since the moment I saw you on the balcony? When I pulled into the parking lot, you were making your way up. I thought you might be able to use some expert advice. Do you mind?"

"If the only thing you offer is advice, no." She rose and turned to study the cliff behind her. She was six, maybe seven feet from the top and she *would* make it on her own. She found a series of handholds and footholds. Stepping forward, she began to climb.

She reached the top, on her own, crawled over the edge and rolled to her back to stare up at the sky. Her legs shook, and her hands burned from the scrapes. Dust and dirt covered her clothes, and she wondered if it had been worthwhile.

Alex extended his hand and pulled her up. "Come on. The best part is just a few feet away." He led her to the edge of the crag.

They looked down on the flat plain.

Low in the sky, the sun touched everything with a soft, gilded tip. The land was gold, and flowering bushes spread across the floor of the valley like a yellow carpet. The sky was a brilliant blue, the rocks a rich deep red. Cars on a distant road flashed like diamonds sprinkled across the earth. Beautiful.

As breathtaking as Lara had imagined it. She dropped to her knees.

Alex joined her.

If Lara sat still and quiet enough, the answers would come to her on the gentle breeze. The view gave her peace, made her feel whole and somehow, a little wiser. After a while, she turned to Alex.

He had one arm looped over a raised knee. The look in his eyes made her heart beat faster.

"Is it everything you'd hoped it to be?" His low voice caressed like warm, gentle fingers.

"Yes." Her gaze raked the land once more, and she couldn't stop the smile. "Yes. It is." She turned back to face him. The wind blew a strand of hair over her mouth.

He tucked it behind her ear. "Good," he said, his gaze fixed on her lips. "I'm glad because it's more than I'd hoped for."

"What did you hope to see?" she asked.

"You. I was hoping to see the real you."

The wind blew the strand of hair back. Alex stroked it away again, his fingers lingering on her cheek. "Since I first saw you, I knew this moment was coming. There was something about you...as if you were on the verge of discovering something incredible. I wanted to be there when you found it." He leaned forward, his voice low, his eyes focused on hers. "What do you see, Lara? What's out there for you?"

She dragged her gaze from his to look at the panoramic landscape. "Answers," she said after a pause. "I think if I can just fly far enough and fast enough, I'll find the answers to all my questions. They're waiting for me to discover them."

"Do you feel powerful?"

"Invincible!" She laughed, tilting her head back to feel the sun's golden kiss on her cheeks.

Alex laughed, too. His rich, low voice stroked her senses like velvet. She loved to hear his voice...laughing...talking...and when he sang, he took her to places she'd only dreamed about. Lara could lose herself in his voice.

"Hang on to that feeling of invincibility," he said. "It'll carry you through many dark days."

She turned to look at him, squinting against the setting sun. His dark eyes were fixed on the distant mountains and a smile hovered, his firm lips tilted slightly. She wanted to touch them, to run her fingers over them while he spoke.

"You make it sound like this will be the only good moment I'll ever have."

"There'll be others. Many others. Now that you know them, you'll seek them out and store them like treasures. When I play, what you hear are moments like these. When you dance, I suspect you'll see them. You'll remember them."

This one was imprinted on her soul. The sun. The cerulean blue sky. The way the breeze lifted Alex's hair. The smile that mirrored what she was feeling deep, down inside. His dark, tanned hands with strong, long fingers. Graceful yet powerful. How could a man's hands say so much about him?

It was a moment carved in time. Everything else seemed to fade. Nothing mattered. Not Brett's stressed state, or Troy and Eliza's marriage. Only this feeling of timelessness…and the man who shared it with her.

"Do you think Juan and Lucia shared moments like this?" she asked.

"I'm sure of it."

His gaze traveled down to her lips. He was so close, he could have kissed her. She wanted him to kiss her, but he didn't. Lara was thankful and a little sad at the same time.

"Now it's time for you to tell me what frightened

you so much on the road today."

~*~

Alex figured he was in for another argument.

Then she released a deep sigh. "I guess I do need to talk to someone." Her gaze focused on the setting sun. "I've seen those men."

"You recognized them?"

"Yes. I think they were there to hurt Christy."

"Christy!" He raised his hand. "Wait. Slow down. A lot more is going on here than just what happened today. Maybe you'd better start at the beginning." He didn't need to act. His surprise was genuine.

She hesitated, perhaps debating how much to tell. What did she have to hide? How deeply was she involved? She'd take risks with herself, he was sure, but certainly not with Christy. Stomping on his apprehension, he forced himself to appear calm.

"I saw the two men from the SUV last night, after I left you. They were in an alley talking to Troy. I didn't get a good look at them in the dark, but I saw their silhouettes and I heard their voices. They wanted Troy to do something illegal."

Alex tensed. "What illegal thing?"

"I don't know, but Troy was furious. He told them straight up he wouldn't do it. He said they had a business transaction he would see fulfilled, but he refused to do anything illegal. He said he wouldn't even consider it and stormed off."

Alex leaned back on his hands. "So they showed up today and threatened his little girl."

"I'm beginning to think so."

"What business transaction does Troy have with

them?" He spoke aloud, more to himself than Lara. He was surprised when she answered.

"I think he borrowed money. Troy's deeply in debt, in over his head with his collectors' pieces. I think...well, I'm afraid he's taking money from the school and Brett's covering for him."

Alex blinked, not sure he'd followed her train of thought. He took a deep breath, trying to trace back her steps. "I don't follow, Lara. Are you telling me funds are missing from the school's accounts?"

"No. But checks are missing, and I'm not even sure Brett knows about them."

"If he doesn't know, how is he covering for Troy?"

"Because Brett is one of my father's most trusted employees. He trusts Brett so much, he gave him a great deal of leeway with the school. But now Brett has gone over-budget and extended the school's finances so far, they're teetering on collapse. Brett is too good a businessman to let that happen. He would never make those kinds of mistakes on his own, and even if he did, he would go straight to my father unless..."

"Unless he was protecting someone else's mistakes."

"Exactly. It's the only thing that makes sense to me."

"Embezzlement is a federal crime, Lara. You don't just cover something like that up—not even for your best friend."

"But there hasn't been any embezzlement that I can see...not yet. Just bad choices. The finest building materials. City permits that should have been contested by our legal department, but Brett gave in and paid the fees so construction wouldn't be held up. The situation got deeper and deeper, and he's been struggling to balance it all out. He cut back where he could—like using a cheaper P.R. firm. He only agreed to hire you because everyone was convinced you'd make the event a success."

A smile twisted across Alex's lips. "And I sabotaged all of his efforts by criticizing the school the first day out."

"Pretty much."

"So where do the checks come in?"

"I was sitting at Brett's desk, resting my head on it and I noticed a space in the ledger, so I poked my finger in there and flipped back the cover. Checks and their carbon sheets had been torn out so neatly, you almost couldn't tell. In fact, if you weren't focusing on it like I was, you wouldn't see it."

"Until the missing checks show up in Fallon's finance department, and Brett's called on the carpet."

Lara sighed with relief. "I'm so glad your mind is thinking like mine. I thought I was being silly, letting my imagination run away with me."

"Being nearly run off the road has nothing to do with your imagination. In fact, I'd say you should be applauded for keeping it together."

"Tell that to my father when you meet him, will you?"

He touched her chin. "I promise."

Her expression made Alex's guilt burn a little hotter.

"The thing that doesn't make any sense to me is why." Her lovely eyes clouded with worry and confusion. "Why would Brett let this go so far, and how could Troy let himself get in debt to people like that in the first place?"

"Setting Troy up would have been easy. Perhaps

Troy used brokers to buy the pieces so he didn't know the true owner. Or the loans could have been bought later, after the sales were done, by someone unscrupulous."

"Or by someone he trusted."

Alex met Lara's gaze. He hadn't appreciated until now how quickly her mind worked. "Do you know someone like that, someone Troy trusts, who might have loaned him money?"

"No. But I can find out."

The determination in her voice set Alex on edge. "I don't want you taking any chances, Lara. These men tried to run us off the road today. They're dangerous. You don't need to get involved."

"I'm already involved. The people I love are in danger and I won't sit by and watch." She turned to face the dipping sun. "I can't believe this is happening...and all because Troy owes someone money when all he has to do is talk to my father."

Another burn of guilt swept through Alex. He couldn't tell Lara how much more there was to the plot without explaining his deception. He couldn't do that. Not yet. Maybe not ever.

He faced the setting sun as the truth he'd been avoiding crept deep into his bones. He'd demanded trust from her, and she'd given it. That and more. But he was holding something back, manipulating her like a puppet after he'd accused everyone she loved and trusted of doing the same thing. He was caught in a web of his own making. He'd been too clever, too smart for his own good.

From the moment he'd met Lara, he'd understood her, bonded with her...and he'd used that bond to get what he wanted. All for the greater good, he'd told himself. And maybe it had been. But in the end, it would cost him. He had the feeling the price would be more than he wanted to pay.

Rising, he extended his hand. "Come on. We need to get going if we want to get off this mountain before dark."

"I have to talk to Troy and tell him I know everything. This has to stop. I won't let Christy be put in harm's way."

Alex gritted his teeth. "Yes, you'll have to talk to him. But not yet. Not just yet."

She turned to him, her blue eyes wide. "Why not?"

Because I need time to follow these leads, to find hard core evidence.

"We need more information."

She studied him and Alex shifted, uncomfortable beneath her gaze.

"If their goal was to scare Troy by threatening Christy, they've done their work." Alex explained. "Now they'll wait to see what Troy does. Christy is safe for the time being. That gives us time."

"Time for what?"

"To discover what they're really after. This was a pretty elaborate setup, Lara. Months of preparation and probably lots of money have gone into this game. Just so they could get money back from Troy? I think something else is going on, and we need to find out what that could be."

"You're probably right. But I don't even know where to begin."

Alex hid his sigh of relief. "Let's start at the school. It seems to be the center of all this."

"OK. We can start now. Everyone's gone." She hurried ahead of him to punch in her code numbers at the door.

Alex looked away, determined to bury his feelings of guilt. Lara was in danger. The sooner he found out the truth, the sooner she would be safe.

As soon as they stepped inside, Lara flipped on a light and headed toward the offices. Halfway there, her phone chirped. "Brett. He's asking me to check the mail room for a letter."

"The school has a mail room?"

She nodded, her back to him as she led the way down the hall. "All my father's offices have one. His business does a lot of shipping and receiving with crates and all. A mailroom is pretty standard."

They walked into a back room with a large loading door for receiving shipments.

While Lara searched the desk for Brett's letter, Alex moved to the back. In one dark corner, he found several wooden crates. They were empty and all shipping labels had been carefully removed, but as Alex stepped closer, something gritted beneath his shoes.

Using the light of his cell phone, he crouched to examine the floor. Dirt. The mailroom was clean everywhere except here, near these crates. He held the cell phone inside the crate and found a pile in one corner. He pinched some of the material between his fingertips. More dirt. Good, red, Southwest dirt. Could it have come from a shipment of ancient Chaco pottery looted from a priceless archaeological site?

"Is there a shipping manifest?" He called to Lara across the room.

"Usually, yes. Packing and shipping is a big deal. It's kind of an important position in my father's company."

"So they wouldn't hire a local?"

"Not likely." Lara continued her search of the desk. "They would want someone with experience, someone they trained."

Alex brushed the dirt off his fingertips as he walked to the desk.

"Here's the manifest." Lara handed him a clipboard.

The list contained shipments for the previous month. Most of the listings were for art equipment and supplies. Only four entries were blank. No weight, contents, or prices were listed. The crates could have contained anything...including illegal Chaco pottery.

At the height of the Anasazi craze, pothunters destroyed valuable sites that might have revealed more information about the ancient Chaco people. Pothunters even desecrated Native American gravesites in search of perfect pieces of fifteen hundred-year-old pottery. Laws were enacted to protect and preserve not only the artifacts, but to prevent the desecration of sacred Native American lands. The laws specifically prohibited the removal and sale of Chaco artifacts from public or Native American lands.

Could this be the threat hanging over Troy's head? Use Fallon Enterprises' resources to ship the illegally obtained artifacts out of the country or they would hurt his daughter. Did Brett know and if he did, how far up the company chain did the knowledge go...all the way to Lara's father? Had Daniel Fallon purposely removed himself from the school for his own protection?

Alex almost didn't want to know the answers. He forced himself to scan the list again, then he looked at the labeled numbers on the backs of the crates across the room…the only numbers with no shipping details.

"I need to know the name of the man in charge of this mailroom." Alex struggled to keep his tone low. "Can you get it for me?"

12

"Alan Chang." Alex tilted his cell phone closer to his mouth and spelled the last name of the mailroom clerk for clarification. Lara had texted the name to him early this morning and he, in turn, had called Immigration and Customs Enforcement Special Agent in Charge, Jason Bowman.

An international advisory and reporting agency, UNESCO had no legal or judicial powers. Alex's usual course of action when working was to liaison with the legal authorities of the country. In the U.S., I.C.E. was the authority, specifically Agent Bowman.

"I'll do a background check on Chang ASAP," Bowman said. "Did you happen to take photos of the crates?"

"No. I didn't want to alert Ms. Fallon. Besides, something bothers me about those crates."

"What do you mean?"

"Too obvious. The crates were sitting right out in the open with the numbers on the back and the manifest on the desk. These criminals have been clever...too clever to leave a trail that obvious. And then there's the anonymous tip."

Bowman was silent for a moment. "Are you thinking it's some kind of a setup?"

"It might be. I'm actually beginning to think the Fallon folks are innocent." *Or at least some of them.*

"You could be right. Let me see what I can find on

this Chang, and I'll get back to you."

"Did you run the check on the license plate number I gave you?"

"Yeah, the black SUV is registered to an Arizona company called Far Sites. An offshore company owns it, but the CEO is a man by the name of Louis Ferone. No priors. No record. But he's considered an expert in Southwest pottery, ancient and modern."

"Sounds like the connection we're looking for."

"Could be. We're checking into it now. In the meantime, be careful. I don't like the attack, especially since it involved the Madrigal child. It's my job to protect antiquities *and* civilians. That includes *you*, my friend. If anything else happens, I'll call a halt to the investigation and bring them all in for questioning."

"If you do, you'll destroy the Fallon School of Art's opening and maybe its chances of success."

"If it prevents someone from being hurt, that's a price we'll have to pay. Be careful." Bowman said. "We'll talk later." He clicked off.

Alex stared into space. He wasn't so sure he was willing to let the school fail, especially since it would destroy Lara. In fact, it would salve his conscience a great deal if he could find a way to make the school a success.

A day, Lord. Just give me another day to make it right.

A noise at the open glass door of the guesthouse broke Alex's prayerful reverie. The small patio outside was empty, but the shadow of a man flickered across the steps. Leaping out the door, Alex crossed the patio and saw Carlos stalking toward the main house.

"How much did you hear?" Alex called out.

Carlos froze and turned slowly. His face was dark red with barely contained emotion. "Enough to know you've returned to your activities with UNESCO."

Alex folded his arms. "Returned? I never stopped."

Carlos's lips thinned into a tight, thin white line. "I assumed you stopped after the incident in Istanbul."

"You assumed wrong."

Alex's efforts in the Turkish capital had resulted in a collection of stolen Syrian antiquities being repatriated to the Syrian government. The angry collector, a Syrian national, attempted to sell the artifacts for arms to support his cause.

Caught by the authorities based on information Alex provided, the Syrian turned on Alex. An army of agents pounced before the culprit was able to inflict any real harm. The incident had little effect on Alex, but apparently had made a big impression on Carlos. Lately, Carlos had been inserting himself in all of Alex's business, and his tolerance was near its breaking point.

"All right, then." Carlos threw his arms out in exasperation. "I *hoped* you would stop putting yourself in danger and focus more on our music."

"Our music?" Anger coiled tightly inside Alex. "I wasn't aware you had written any of the pieces we perform. In fact, in spite of my constant encouragement and suggestions, you have failed to create any of your own work."

The deep red color of Carlos's face drained, leaving him pale.

In that moment, Alex recognized the truth. He had never met a musician who didn't play around with music a little, creating his own compositions, or at least bits of songs. Carlos had none. His blanched features confirmed a suspicion that had been growing in Alex's mind for a long while.

Carlos performed not for his love of music, but for a love of fame. He'd attached himself to Alex and had taken an acute interest in all his actions...even to the point of spying and listening to his conversations.

Alex could not permit the situation to continue. "This is a conversation we've had far too frequently to repeat again, Carlos. You need to develop as an artist. I will see to it that you have time."

"What...what do you mean?"

"After this engagement, our association will be at an end. I will contact my lawyers immediately and have them draw up the papers to end our partnership." Without another word, he spun and walked back into the guesthouse.

~*~

The long-awaited morning of horseback riding finally arrived. Lara rose early to ask Brett the name of the mailroom clerk. When she texted the info to Alex, he replied that he would not be able to ride with them, due to some business. Disappointed, and determined not to do the same to Christy, Lara headed up to the main house.

The car ride to the stables wound its way through a narrow, twisting canyon. It reminded Lara of the earlier incident. She was relieved when they turned off the road into a dirt driveway.

The driver parked in front of a sprawling ranch house.

Two young people with sandy-colored hair came out. The girl appeared to be around sixteen, the boy closer to Christy's age. He went to the back of the limo and walked around it, but the girl headed straight for them.

"Hi. I'm Melissa Holt, and this is my brother, Tommy. Are you Christy?"

"Yes, that's me."

"Great!" The girl smiled. "We've been waiting for you." She gestured to the house. "My dad's in the office. By the time you've finished signing the papers, we'll have the horses ready."

Dan Holt had the same sandy hair and healthy outdoor look of his children. As Lara paid and signed the waivers, Dan chatted about the trail and informed them his children would be their guides. Within minutes, they were back outside.

Four horses were tied to the corral railings. Tommy walked around them, tugging cinches and testing saddles.

"So are we ready?" Melissa asked.

"All set." Lara guided Christy to the first horse.

"Have you ever ridden before?" Melissa addressed Christy.

"I used to ride all the time, but I've been sick for a while."

Tommy murmured under his breath and rolled his eyes.

Melissa sent him a piercing glare. "Ignore him." She spoke directly to Christy as if Tommy and Lara had disappeared. "He's into cars, right now. He *thinks* he wants to be a race car driver, but my dad *makes* him work here when he's out of school, so he acts like a jerk and tries to make the rest of us miserable, too."

Christy glanced his way. "He can be as big a jerk as he wants as he long as he lets me ride."

Melissa laughed. "I like your attitude, Christy.

We're going to have a great time today." She winked as she helped Christy mount.

Watching the two girls made Lara smile.

They took a trail that wound into the mountains before it began to climb. They entered a narrow canyon with high, sandy cliffs on each side. Melissa took the lead with Christy following, then Lara, and Tommy in the rear. The girls talked, Melissa pointing out land features, and Christy responding in kind, although she glanced back often with smiles for Lara.

The narrow confines of the canyon made Lara uncomfortable. Especially after shadows fell across the trail from above. She chalked it up to a case of nerves.

A while later, Tommy called out. "Hang on a minute."

They brought their horses to a halt and looked back.

Tommy's gaze trailed along the rim of the cliffs.

"What is it?" Melissa asked.

"Don't know. For a minute, I thought someone was up there."

Shivers rippled down Lara's spine. So it wasn't just her imagination! She studied the cliffs and the trail ahead. If someone were up there, what were they planning? Pinned as the four of them were in this narrow canyon, someone could easily shove boulders or rocks down on them—even swoop down and snatch Christy right out of her hands. How would she stop them? What could she do?

"I guess I was wrong," Tommy said. "There's nothing there. Let's move on."

Someone *was* up there, stalking them, waiting for the right moment. Lara's gaze swept continually over the trail ahead and back to the edges. She pulled out her cell phone to call Alex, but she had no reception.

By the time the trail became an open space, Lara was a bundle of nerves. Now that they were clear of the cliffs, she could see the ranch house ahead. Some of her tension eased. But she was more than ready for the ride to end. Trying not to convey her concerns to the young people, she took several long breaths.

When they finally reached the ranch house, Daniel Holt was waiting for them. "How was the ride?"

Christy responded enthusiastically. She and Melissa made plans for a return visit.

Lara looked back at the path and the mountain, wondering if she'd let her fears get the best of her.

"What do you think, Lara? Would it be all right?"

"I—we'll see," she replied with a quick smile, covering her lack of attention.

"If Lara can't make it next week, maybe my mom can. She loves to ride too," Christy said.

"Great. I'll put it in the books." Melissa waved and headed to the office while Tommy led the horses towards the corral. He didn't say a word, but Lara wasn't so worried that she missed the quick glance he sent back in Christy's direction.

Christy didn't miss it either, and Lara's smile slipped out, sneaking right past her worries. Everything she'd hoped would happen in this outing had come true. Christy had discovered she could still be physical. She'd had fun and even met some kids close to her age. Lara wanted to be pleased, but her suspicions took the shine off her happiness. Thankfully, Christy seemed completely unaware.

In the limo, Christy started to chatter. Still pumped up, she carried on and on about the horses, the beautiful trail, so different from the trails in New

York and Central Park. Melissa was wonderful and Tommy was a jerk, but her voice held a certain tone that Lara couldn't miss.

"I've never really been into car races," Christy said. "If it's so interesting, maybe I should check it out."

Lara couldn't help smiling again and eased back into her seat. Had she let her emotions get the best of her?

An SUV came alongside on the left and slowed, pacing the limo.

"Hey," Christy called out. "That looks like the car that almost ran us off the mountain!"

The SUV shot ahead of them. When it was a couple of car lengths in front, it signaled, and pulled over to the side.

"Wow." Christy's voice was low. "That was weird. Why do you suppose they had to get in front of us and then pulled over to the side? It was almost like they wanted to make sure we noticed them."

"Oh, they probably just had a problem and had to turn off." But Lara was convinced Christy spoke the truth. The men in the car wanted to make sure Lara knew they'd been followed all the way from the trail.

~*~

Lara left Christy to relate their adventure to Eliza and slipped away with a wave. She was desperate to talk to Alex but preferred to do it from the security of her own room. Almost running down the path to her bungalow, she pushed open the door and stopped. Suitcases sat in the doorway, and her dad stood in the center of the room. Argument and differences forgotten, Lara flew into his arms.

"Hello, sweetheart." His voice gave Lara so much comfort it brought tears to her eyes.

"Dad, I'm so glad to see you."

"I know. I'm sorry I stayed away so long. You were right. You were so right. I was avoiding coming here. I let you and Brett and Troy take responsibility for your mother's school. I was wrong, and I'm sorry."

Lara was so surprised, she laughed out loud and raised her head to look into her father's face. "So Rupert Townsend was right. He said plain talk was effective with you."

"Townsend is here?" Her dad gave a shake of his head. "It figures. I should have known he'd try to horn in on your mom's school."

Frowning, Lara leaned even farther back. "Don't be so hard on him. He's agreed to invest a lot of money."

"I doubt that will happen now that I've made a showing. It would be just like him to pull out at the last minute. It's typical of his antics. Sometimes I think his main goal in life is to create trouble for me."

"Townsend doesn't need to create trouble, Dad. We have enough of it on our own." She couldn't keep the worry out of her tone.

Gripping her hands, her father studied her face. "Let's sit down," he said at last. "I think this is going to take a while."

After they were seated, Lara told him about Troy's money problems, the missing checks, Brett's cover-up and even about the SUV. When she'd finished, her dad shook his head.

"I knew there were issues, but I had no idea…" He shook his head again. "Lara, I can't believe you've been handling this all on your own. I'm sorry I abandoned you."

"It's OK, Dad. You're here now."

At his doubtful expression, she grasped his hands. "Really, it is. In fact, I think it's been good for me to sort through things on my own. I needed…"

"The chance to grow up." Her dad's quietly spoken words touched Lara.

"I grew up a long time ago, Dad. I needed to test my capabilities."

"And you've surpassed both our expectations, I think."

"Yes," she said with a little smile. "I guess I surprised myself a little, too. But I'm not finished. There's more that needs to be done."

She told him about Alex's concerns about the school and its curriculum. "He was so right, Dad. We need to provide this wonderful environment for all children, not just the wealthy ones. You can't believe the incredible work I've seen. So many children with unbelievable talent…and equal difficulties…even special needs. I was overwhelmed by the desire to do something."

Her father nodded his head slowly. "I see. And does Alex feel the same way?"

Confused by her dad's hesitation, she said, "No. But I'm firmly convinced this is the direction the school needs to take."

"Brett mentioned Summers's speech and his interest in you."

Understanding filtered through Lara and dread seeped in. "I see. Brett doesn't even know about the missing checks, but he has time to tell you about my relationship with Alex. Is Brett the director of the school or my watchdog, Dad? It seems to me he has his own issues to deal with without butting into mine."

Dad held up his hands. "Whoa, whoa. Slow down. Brett's your friend, and he's concerned. He has a right to be. Apparently, this Summers doesn't have a very good reputation where the ladies are concerned."

Lara shook her head. "Well, fortunately I'm not falling in love with his reputation. I'm falling in love with the real man." The words were out before she even realized she said them.

Her father froze.

So did Lara. She caught her breath. Was it true? Was she falling in love with Alex? Possibly. Maybe. Yes. She looked up into her father's concerned expression.

"Honey, those words don't fill me with confidence."

Lara drew her breath in slowly, calmly. "Dad, you just said you were impressed with what I've accomplished and handled. Can't you give me some credit in this arena, too? I haven't done anything foolish, and I'm not going to. But Alex and I deserve the opportunity to see where that leads, don't you think?"

Her father's lips thinned into a tight white line and for a minute, Lara thought he was going to argue. Then he lifted her hand to his lips and kissed it. "Yes, you do. Just promise me you'll be careful. I don't think I could stand it if my little girl got her heart broken her first time out."

Lara laughed. "It's not exactly my first time out, Dad, but I do promise to be careful."

"Good." He patted the hand he'd just kissed. "Now, where do we go from here?" He gazed into the distance. "Tonight is the grand finale, the party where Brett and Troy unveil the donor's plaques and make their last pitch for sponsors. Everything has to go without a hitch so there's no time to talk. We'll just have to sort all these problems out tomorrow. In the meantime, I'll give you an hour to get rid of the horse smell, and then I'd like to see this building my money bought."

"One more thing, Dad. Since this is the last night, I'd like to make a pitch for my underprivileged children. Do I have your permission to move forward with what I had in mind?"

He studied her for a moment, and then lifted her to her feet. "Go for it. I'd like to see what you've got."

The twinkle in his eyes made her laugh out loud. "Then make it half an hour. I can't wait to get started!"

13

"We've got an APB out for the arrest of Alan Chang." Alex could barely hear Bowman's voice over the crowded foyer of the school.

Early arrivals for the cocktail party were happily milling about, drinking and snapping up the refreshments passed around by waiters wearing white smocks and painter's berets.

Alex stepped onto the school's back deck, away from the noise. "That was quick. Obviously you found something in his background check."

"Just a gambling addiction with debts in every state of the nation."

Alex was silent as the new information clicked into place. "So you think he needs money in the worst way. Bad enough to betray his employer?"

"Or he's being blackmailed by someone else to betray his employer."

"Pressured like Troy," Alex murmured, almost to himself.

"It fits the pattern. We wanted to pull Chang in for questioning but he didn't return to work. Left for lunch and never came back. We've had a man at his apartment all afternoon and he didn't show up there, either."

"You think something...or someone tipped him off."

"Or his dangerous friends decided to take him out

of the equation."

A cool evening breeze rippled over Alex's loose performance shirt, sending chills down his back.

"The stakes just got higher, my friend," Bowman said. "I don't like it. If not for you, I'd pull out all the stops and interrupt this event no matter how important it is."

"That kind of action would destroy the school's opening."

"Maybe. But the longer we wait, the colder the trail gets and the more time these crooks have to cover their tracks. I have a bad feeling about it."

"If you're worried about the Fallon folks making a run for it, I don't think that's going to happen." Alex glanced back through the glass doors at the receiving line where Daniel, Troy, Brett, and Eliza were greeting the incoming guests.

There was no sign of Lara, but he needed to find her, needed to talk to her before it was too late. The knot was unraveling. If he didn't find a way to tell her the truth soon, he never would. "Daniel Fallon showed up this afternoon," Alex told Bowman. "He seems to have energized the group. For the first time, they seem to be pulling together, focusing on the school and its future."

"Could be," Bowman said slowly. "And then it could be Fallon's arrival coincides with Chang's disappearance."

Another chill swept up Alex's back. This one had nothing to do with the cold air. Was he wrong? Had his emotions colored his judgment? If he spoke with Lara, would she warn her father and destroy the investigation?

If Lara found out Alex had deceived her before he

could tell her, she'd feel betrayed. If her family and friends were involved in this crime, she'd feel the same way. Either way, the woman he was falling in love with would be hurt...and that meant he would be, too.

"We're processing a search warrant for Chang's apartment," Bowman continued. "As soon as it comes through, we're going in. If we see any signs of violence, school or no school, we're going straight to Fallon's place. In the meantime, keep your eyes and ears open. If you notice any change or sign of trouble, call me immediately. This is getting too dangerous."

Alex closed his eyes.

"Do you hear me, Summers?"

"Yes, yes, I hear you." Alex punched the End button on his phone. Any hope of a future with Lara might have just ended.

~*~

Lara stepped back to study the chalk drawing centered in the simple frame resting on an easel.

Not bad, especially for such a rush job! Unless of course, they look on the back and see the duct tape.

Lara smiled. With her father's permission, she'd taken the initiative. While Troy and Brett greeted her dad, she'd slipped into Brett's office and removed some of the samples of art submitted by underprivileged children. Making a choice had been tough, but in the end, she'd picked this chalk landscape, an incredible city scene in pencil, and the piano CD by a young girl in a wheelchair.

She'd hurried into the mailroom to gather the supplies she needed. Fortunately, no one asked any questions.

The mailroom clerk had not come back from lunch and that had sent the rest of the employees in a tizzy, trying to reach him and fill in the gaps. They were responsible for mounting and presenting the donor plaques, and with the lead clerk gone, turmoil reigned.

Lara grabbed what she needed and made her escape without too much notice.

Then she'd hurried back to the house and dressed for the event in record time. She returned to the school late, once again avoiding unnecessary questions and explanations. She set the easels in a small passageway between the large common room and the smaller room where Alex and Carlos were scheduled to play after the presentation of the plaques. Guests would pass by this area, see the pieces, and hear the piano sonata playing. They couldn't miss it. They'd be intrigued and…hopefully…ask questions.

With one last glance around her display, Lara smoothed her hands over her hips. She'd chosen a little black dress with straight lines, short sleeves and a slight flare at the knees. She loved the simple, clean lines and had slicked her hair into a small knot at the back for the same effect. She was ready.

Stepping out of the passage into the crowd, she searched for Alex. All afternoon an idea had been dancing around in her head. He'd asked about the mail clerk and now the man had gone missing. It seemed too coincidental. She suspected he knew something he wasn't telling.

Most of the guests had arrived. Her father chatted and laughed with a group of friends near the door. Brett stood slightly apart from the group, looking like a whipped dog…or someone with a guilty conscience.

Her father, Brett, and Troy had talked for hours

this afternoon behind closed doors. Judging from Brett's hangdog expression, it hadn't gone his way.

Eliza stood across the room listening to an older lady. Lara's friend appeared distracted, barely paying attention. She reached for a glass of champagne as a waiter went by, clearly disturbed. Obviously, Christy had told her mother about their second encounter with the black SUV.

Troy stood close by, looking relaxed and calm with a group of donors. He acted as if he didn't have a care in the world and that puzzled Lara. Of them all, he had reason to be the most concerned.

Milly Johansson was decked out in a long, black skirt and flowing top. She gave a shy little wave.

Delighted, Lara hurried toward her. "You're supposed to be in L.A."

"We were. But our drummer slammed his hand in a car door and the recording sessions had to be postponed. I wanted to come back, so...here we are." She gave an embarrassed shrug. "I feel bad about his injury, but I was really glad to make it back for this."

"Me, too. Come with me. I have something to show you." Hooking her arm through Milly's, she led her to the small passage and her carefully chosen art pieces.

As they walked, Milly said, "I met your dad. He's..."

"Formidable," Lara finished.

"Yeah. He certainly exudes power."

"And my mother shimmered like some precious metal." Lara looked up at the ceiling. "She glowed. When the two of them walked into a room, all eyes were on them. They were larger than life, and then...there was me." Lara was surprised at how little the words hurt.

"You have your own special gifts," Milly said quietly.

Lara smiled and squeezed the other woman's arm. "I know. You were right about that. In fact, you were right about a lot of things. I've become involved in the school, and I think it's made a difference. Take a look." She gestured to the display she'd created and paused.

"Wow," Milly said. "This is something my husband and I could really support."

"You think so?" Lara asked.

"Totally. We have a thing for misfit kids. Go figure," she said. "And I have a good feeling about this. We'll have to pray about it, of course, but…"

"Oh, Milly, I'm so glad we met. You're special to me already. Our talks have meant a lot. You've been right about so many things. I even met a dark-haired stranger."

Milly studied Lara's face before she nodded. "I've seen the way you look at Alejandro Summers. Do you love him?"

"I think I'm beginning to." Lara stopped.

"But…" Milly prompted.

"But…I'm not sure I know what love is. I believed I loved Brett, but that faded beside what I feel for Alex. He makes my soul sing, and I can't wait to hear what he has to say next. The world sparkles when I'm with him."

"But…" Milly said again.

Lara sighed. "I loved my mom…too much. And my dad. Everything I did, I did to please them. And then, just like that, my mom was gone and my powerful dad was a shadow of himself. I was almost a grown woman and I didn't know what to do or where to turn. It took me a long time to heal and get on with my life. I'm not sure I want that kind of love again."

Milly grasped her hand. "You don't. You want a different kind of love, a fulfilling, secure love. It's time you experienced God's love. Find out what He created you to be, who He wants you to be, and what He has planned for you. Then you'll truly know your own heart, and it will be safe to follow it."

"I'm not sure what that means, or how I'll do it." Lara managed a little smile. "But given your track record of good advice, I'll try to figure it out."

"Deal." Milly held out her hand for a shake.

Lara took it, and they both laughed.

"Come on." Milly grasped Lara's arm this time. "I want to tell Avery about this."

The whole time Milly related the story to her husband, Lara searched the crowd for Alex. When she finally spotted him, he had just greeted a new arrival at the door, a distinguished older gentleman Lara didn't recognize.

Thinking of older gentlemen reminded Lara she hadn't seen Rupert Townsend. She searched the room. He was not in attendance. Perhaps her father had been right. If her father was involved, it was possible Rupert wouldn't follow through with his support. But Milly and Avery might donate to the school and the children for the *right* reasons.

Alex and his companion joined them. "Lara, this is Doctor Theodore Jerome. Dr. Jerome is one of the leading researchers in multiple learning." He looked at her as if the phrase should mean something.

"I'm sorry. What's multiple learning?"

"Chemistry from paint mixtures. Sculpting through math... It's the term used for different ways of teaching."

Lara gasped and extended her hand. "Doctor! What a pleasure to meet you."

"What's more, Lara," Alex didn't give her time to finish the introduction. "He's just been awarded a substantial research grant to study multiple learning."

"Yes, Ms. Fallon, and from what Professor Summers tells me, you need a curriculum. If I can create a curriculum for your students that meets the specifications of our study, we might be able to use Fallon students as our first subjects."

Lara was speechless. All she could do was to grasp Alex around the neck and kiss him.

At first, his arms wrapped around her, and he returned the kiss. But then, as if remembering where they were and who was watching, he grasped her arms and tugged them loose. He looked away from Lara so quickly, it surprised her.

Was this the man who'd told her he didn't worry about what others thought or said?

"Of course," Alex said, unable to meet her gaze. "I'll have to return to Madrid and my work in a few days. But I've offered to help, Dr. Jerome, long distance if I can."

Why had he said that? Was he trying to remind her he had a career and a life elsewhere? That he couldn't stay, couldn't commit to the school or to her?

Lara understood. The future was a blank slate and she had no plans or expectations. Conversation about the school carried on, and soon, she was caught up.

The group was still chatting when Brett announced Alex's performance would take place in a few moments.

Avery walked to the passageway, motioning for

Milly and Lara to follow. "I think *our* project needs attention." Avery began to discuss the art. People stopped to listen as he pointed out features on the easels and noted the music.

Dr. Jerome asked questions and talked of multiple learning techniques. Everyone who passed paused to listen.

A gentleman from a large computer corporation spoke up. "This sounds exactly like the type of program we want to fund. We have a substantial investment, and we're looking to start an endowment."

From behind her husband's back, Milly caught Lara's gaze. Her friend winked and Lara couldn't hold back a small laugh. More people joined the conversation or asked for information. They created such a stir, the group was still gathered in the passage when Alex and Carlos began to play.

The sweet strains of Flamenco music captured Lara's attention immediately. The group broke up.

Lara went into the performance room, stopping at the back, deep in the shadows. She leaned against the wall and listened. Across the room, Alex caught her with his gaze. His music conjured new memories, a fiery sunset, the burn of her muscles as she climbed, the rough texture of a rock wall, and a limitless horizon with red rocks and cars sparkling like diamonds in the distance.

Still, Alex's music had an undertone of a gypsy campfire, of Juan and Luisa, lovers separated forever. Had the spell of the guitar trapped her? Would the music remind her of a love so sweet, so tender, and over too soon?

She listened to the rest of the concert with bittersweet feelings, wondering if this would be her last night with Alex. She tried to absorb and remember every nuance, how his long fingers spread over the width of the guitar. How a few strands of dark hair fell over his brow when he strummed. How his gaze softened every time he saw her. Too soon, the concert was over.

People rose to their feet clapping, rushing forward to greet Alex and Carlos.

Alex didn't come towards her.

Lara felt bereft. Abandoned. She and Alex had exchanged no promises, no words of commitment. Nothing had really passed between them...except an explosion of chemistry, and a bond that seemed to reach so deep, it touched their souls.

Lara firmed her shoulders. Something *did* spark to life between them. Something unique. Important. She wouldn't let it end so easily. She leaned back against the wall, deeper into the shadows, hoping no one would see her so she could find a quiet moment to speak to Alex.

He placed La Guitarra in its case. Carlos did the same with his guitar. They worked silently, placing the other guitars in cases and folding their stands. The security men stood nearby so they could escort Carlos to the van to transport him, the valuable guitars, and the equipment back to the house.

Alex handed the case with La Guitarra to Carlos. He extended his hand to Carlos. Carlos stared at Alex's hand for a moment. Then he turned and left Alex standing there, hand still outstretched. With a shake of his head, Alex said something to Mike McGraff, the head of security, before he turned and caught sight of Lara.

"There you are." Brett stepped out of the passage

behind Lara. "Your father's looking everywhere for you. Seems you started quite a little sensation tonight. He's in a hot and heavy discussion with a gentleman by the name of Dr. Jerome, and he'd like you to join them."

Alex had approached and stood just slightly apart, as if waiting his turn to speak with Lara.

Brett turned to him. "You too, Alex. Some serious brainstorming is going on, and they'd like you two to be a part of it." Brett gestured Alex ahead, and then took Lara's arm, holding her back. "Good job, Lara." A genuine smile lit Brett's features. "I haven't seen your dad this pleased and excited about a project since he lost your mom."

"Really?"

"Really. He's proud of you Lara, which…is more than I can say about myself. I'm a big disappointment to him."

"I'm sure Dad didn't say that."

"He didn't have to. I know I blew this. I don't need him to smack my hands with the ruler to admit it."

"Brett…I…I don't know what to say."

"There's nothing you can say. I'm a big enough boy to take responsibility for my actions."

His actions? Was Brett more responsible than she realized? Was he trying to tell her something?

He glanced down the passage to a group seated in a large circular sofa set, avidly discussing students, funds and dormitories. Brett ducked his head. "I just…well, there might not be time for me to say this later. I just want you to know your friendship has meant a lot to me and I…well, I'm proud of you, too." He squeezed her arm and tugged her forward to join the group.

Her father gestured to a seat and she sat down, her mind churning. First Alex's strange behavior and now Brett's. Both of them were as tense as electric wires. Their attitudes put her on edge.

The plans for her program were taking shape. This should have been a night of triumph. Instead, she felt as tightly wound as one of Alex's guitar strings. She tried to participate in the conversation while keeping an eye on the important men in her life.

Brett stared at the front door as if he'd like nothing better than to run away.

Alex kept dragging his cell phone out of his pocket and checking the screen. After the fifth time, he looked around the group and interrupted. "Forgive me. I'm expecting a call from Madrid I must take, if you'll excuse me." He exchanged good-byes and made promises to contact everyone...except Lara.

Lara quietly excused herself and followed him to the front of the building. "Alex, wait."

He froze, his back tense, shoulders sagging in defeat. When he turned, his features wore an almost pained look.

"Alex, what's going on? Why are you behaving so strangely tonight?"

He grasped her hands. "I wish I could tell you. I wish I could explain it all, but I can't. Not right now. Not this way."

"You can't tell me? Aren't you the man who said he didn't have time for gossip or falsehoods? Aren't you the one who said life was too short to try and meet other people's expectations?"

He kissed her fingertips. "Yes, I am that man. And I still believe it, but I simply can't talk about this right now."

She frowned, trying to understand. "Alex, are you trying to tell me goodbye?"

"No! No, I'm trying…" He broke off. "Promise me, Lara, no matter what happens, you'll remember these last few days have meant more to me…" His phone buzzed.

Lara stared at him, trying to understand, hesitant to promise…she didn't know what.

He gave her a little shake. "Promise me?"

She nodded.

He kissed her forehead, and then hurried toward his car and drove away.

Lara stumbled back to the group. The conversation was finally beginning to wind down.

Brett rose and began to turn off the lights of the school as Troy and her father made arrangements to meet with Jerome to draw up papers and plans.

An oddly silent Brett finally said goodnight to the cleanup crew and security, and they all climbed into the limo. Troy and Lara's father were animated, pleased with the event and the evening.

Brett still acted liked a trapped animal longing for escape. He'd moved his things into a smaller room at the main house so her father could have the other bedroom in the guesthouse.

The limo dropped Brett and Troy off.

"I'm not tired, Lara. I believe jet lag hasn't hit me."

Lara kissed him goodnight and went to her room. She could feel the cold of something terrible seeping into her bones. Maybe a hot shower would help. Even the intense heat of the hair dryer after her shower did nothing to impact the ice in her veins, the certainty that something bad was about to happen. She put on lounge pants and a T-shirt and eased into her bed to stare up at the ceiling.

This aching cold reminded her of the months after her mother died…when home turned into an empty, alien place of sorrow. Everything she'd gained, everything she valued in the last few years seemed to be slipping through her fingers, sending her back to those dark days. She could feel the panic rising inside her, and she squeezed her eyes shut. "Please…" she whispered out loud. She didn't even know what she was asking.

But He did. He always knew, and He'd always been with her. He brought her out of the accident, through the surgery and the long, drawn out healing process. He brought her here and gave her a new beginning and even a purpose. He had never abandoned her, and He never would.

The panic began to seep away. The tension eased out of her stomach. She was not alone and for the first time in a long while, she sensed His presence. Taut muscles began to ease. Her eyes closed. Her breath slipped through her lips in a sigh.

The phone connected to the main house rang, jolting her. Her father answered, and then gave an exclamation.

Lara's pulse jumped. She leapt out of bed, ran to her door and opened it. "What is it? What's happened?"

Her father turned to her, his features a mixture of shock and confusion. "La Guitarra is missing. They think it's been stolen."

14

Lara followed her father as he hurried across the compound toward the main house. She tugged the corded sweater she'd thrown over her shoulders and glanced up at a sky full of stars. The first night she'd arrived in Sedona everything had seemed so bright and promising. Now those stars didn't seem so welcoming or so twinkly. Now they looked like bright chips of ice in a frozen black wasteland. Those dismal imaginings made her pull the sweater tighter.

The house lights blazed across the way and several dark sedans were parked outside.

"The police are already here," she murmured.

"Those aren't police cars. They look like Federal employee vehicles." His features were set and hard.

"You mean Federal as in F.B.I.?"

"More like I.C.E. It's the division of Homeland Security dealing with stolen artifacts."

Lara tripped in surprise.

Her father grabbed her elbow and guided her at a faster pace.

They entered the foyer. Two men in suits stood guard at the door of the guitar room. They weren't part of the regular security team. One of the men pointed them toward the large family room. They could hear voices, hushed and subdued, like the sounds at a funeral.

Everyone was already there, including Mike

McGraff, the head of their security. Even Christy was awake and sat silent next to Eliza on the couch. Troy had his arm stretched across the back of the sofa to enclose both his wife and his daughter. Brett and Carlos stood at the back of the room. Brett still wore his increasingly familiar hangdog expression and Carlos paced back and forth, clearly agitated.

Alex stood across the room. His features looked bewildered...pained.

Lara wanted to put her arms around him.

A man in a suit greeted them. "Mr. Fallon, Ms. Fallon, now you're here, we can begin. Please have a seat." He gestured to a chair next to Troy. "I'm Special Agent in Charge, Jason Bowman. I'll be handling this investigation. As you are all aware, La Guitarra is missing. Mr. Summers returned home approximately," he glanced at his watch, "forty-five minutes ago and discovered the guitar sitting on the weight-sensor was not La Guitarra. A subsequent search of the room and preliminary search of the house was fruitless. The guitar has not been located. The security camera, as well as the lock on the outside door, appear to have been tampered with. We have teams coming to help with the investigation. We'll take fingerprints and conduct a more thorough search of the house, but while we wait, I have a few questions. We'll be speaking with each of you individually, but right now, I need a sequence of events."

He turned to Eliza. "Mrs. Madrigal, you arrived home first?"

"Yes, I left right after the donor presentations, before the concert. I was worried about Christy." Immediately, Eliza's gaze shot to Troy, as if she thought she'd spoken out of turn.

Troy smiled and patted her hand.

"We'll talk more about that later." Agent Bowman sounded as if he already knew about the reason Eliza was worried. How could he know about the attacks?

"The next to arrive at the house was Mr. Bertoleo with the security team," Agent Bowman continued. "I assume you secured the guitars in the room and everything was normal."

Carlos nodded, but Mike said, "Not quite. Mr. Bertoleo cut his hand and was bleeding. After we closed the room, he went to the bathroom to find something to clean it with and I checked the thermostat."

"The thermostat?"

"Mr. Bertoleo thought the room was unusually cold."

At Agent Bowman's puzzled expression Alex said, "All guitars are susceptible to extremes in temperature. It impacts the wood, the strings, everything. La Guitarra is especially susceptible because of its age."

"I see." Bowman addressed his question to Mike. "Was there a difference in the thermostat?"

"Yes. The thermostat was flashing...as if it had had a power outage. I was concerned, so I went to the control room to check on the security equipment. Mr. Bertoleo returned and asked me to open the room for him so he could retrieve his guitars."

"You took your personal guitars out of the secure room?" Agent Bowman asked, surprise tingeing his tone. "Why?"

Carlos shifted. "I am to leave early in the morning. I have arranged a car to pick me up for my flight back to Spain."

Bowman turned to Alex. "This isn't your usual

routine."

Alex shrugged. "Carlos and I have ended our partnership. Last night was our last performance."

Bowman knew Alex's routine so well. How? Lara's puzzlement grew.

"Our routine is not as important as La Guitarra," Carlos exclaimed. "Every minute we waste is another minute for the thief to escape. You know the first twenty-four hours are essential to the recovery of a stolen object. Soon La Guitarra will disappear into the abyss of a private collection, and she will be lost to the world. You must do something besides talk, Agent Bowman."

Agent Bowman didn't react. "Thank you for the advice, Mr. Bertoleo. I think we are all aware of the dangers." He turned back to Mike. "After you retrieved the guitars and Mr. Bertoleo left, you returned to the security room."

Mike nodded. "Yes. We determined there had been a power outage on that line and one of the cameras was down."

"But none of the alarms went off."

"No. Only one line seemed to be impacted and if it's a minor fluctuation, it won't set them off. They'll usually reset with no problems, but the camera didn't. By the time we traced out the problem to the power grid, Mr. Madrigal arrived home."

"But you didn't discuss the power outage with him."

"We decided not to create an alarm for a simple power fluctuation. The door was still secure and we believed the main alarm, the weight sensor on which the guitar was placed, had not been affected."

"But you were wrong, and you discovered the

discrepancy when Mr. Summers arrived."

Mike nodded. "Yes. He went into the room and ascertained a switch had been made. The guitar on the sensor was not La Guitarra."

Agent Bowman nodded. "The switch was made between the time you and Mr. Bertoleo left and returned?"

"Yes. We did an immediate surveillance of the grounds and the house. We found that the outer balcony door had been tampered with, but there was nothing on the other cameras and no signs outside."

"Then you informed the authorities?"

Mike nodded.

"I think that answers all my questions," Bowman said.

"But not mine." Lara's father's tone was firm. "I'd like to know how a team from I.C.E. got here even before the local police. I just made the call to your organization this afternoon."

Startled by her father's new information, Lara stared at him. He'd called I.C.E.?

For the first time, Agent Bowman looked uncomfortable and shot a quick glance at Alex. "We...were conducting an investigation so we were already in the area."

"That doesn't explain how you arrived so quickly tonight."

Agent Bowman hesitated again.

"I called them," Alex said. "I knew they were close because I had just been in Agent Bowman's company."

A shocked silence filled the room.

Lara's heart did a stutter step.

"In other words, Mr. Summers, while you've been a guest here in this house, you've been secretly investigating my family." Her father's deep, troubled voice set Lara's nerves a-jangle.

She stopped breathing as she watched Alex. Waiting. Hoping….

Slowly, he nodded. Lara gasped as the ground fell out from beneath her.

~*~

Wearily, Alex looked out the window. Light oozed into the sky on the horizon, announcing dawn's rapid approach. Daniel Fallon would be the last member of the party to be privately interviewed. Hopefully, he would provide more insight than the others. The investigation was not progressing…at least not to Alex's satisfaction.

When Lara had entered the room, she'd refused to even look at him. He ached to take her aside…to try to explain. But what could he say? He'd pulled personal information out of her. She'd shared intimate details of her life, and all the while he'd lied to her. Nothing he could say would make it all right.

Bowman took great pains to point out to Lara that if not for Alex, he would have closed the school's ceremonies early and perhaps ruined its reputation. However, if they'd shut down the ceremony the authorities would have been in the house and at the school. La Guitarra might not have been stolen.

Alex's commitment to the Fallon School of Art may have lost him his most valued possession.

The information didn't seem to impact her feelings. She continued to avoid all contact with him, leaving the room without a word or a backward glance.

He'd lost La Guitarra and Lara. Everything of value in his life.

Daniel Fallon situated himself in a chair across from Bowman. They exchanged a few words before Bowman said, "When did you first realize there were problems with your operation here in Sedona?"

Fallon took a deep breath. "About three weeks ago. Eliza called me and asked to borrow a substantial amount of money. She was very secretive about it. Requested that I not ask any questions or mention it to Troy or Brett. She said she'd been helping out at the school's office and had taken some checks, but she wouldn't use them without my permission."

"She admitted taking the checks?"

"Yes. She said she didn't want Troy or Brett to know she was borrowing the money. I understood Eliza well enough to know she was protecting one of them, most likely Troy. I suspected he had financial troubles."

"Why?"

"I've known Troy for thirty years," Fallon said with a slight smile. "He's a brilliant artist, but a lousy business man. I suspected he'd overextended his finances with this masterpiece." He gestured to their surroundings.

"Did you give Mrs. Madrigal the money?"

"I asked her to wait. Said I had to rearrange my finances. She said it would give her time to finish some glass work and as soon as it sold, she would pay me back."

"What did you do afterwards?"

"Just what I said. I looked over the school's books and realized there was trouble. Brett had lost control and the school was over budget."

"That was three weeks ago, yet you did nothing to correct the situation."

Fallon shrugged his shoulders. "Brett is one of my finest young employees. The school was a training field for him, the opportunity to learn. I wanted to give him the chance to pull it together and make it work. I didn't realize at the time there were outside influences working against him."

"What outside influences?"

"Permits being slowed and in some cases denied." Fallon features hardened as he said the last. "It takes a lot of money to influence government officials. Then when I arrived here, I found out someone had tried to force Troy into receiving unmarked shipments."

"How?"

"An unscrupulous dealer arranged the sale of Troy's valuable antiquities with an anonymous buyer. It's not unusual for a buyer to want to remain unknown and the papers on the items were all in order, so Troy didn't suspect anything. But then the seller offered Troy a deal. The seller agreed to carry a loan for Troy until after the opening of the school. Troy was short on money and thought the opportunity was perfect. Once the deal was made, however, the seller sent men to collect the money early. Of course, Troy didn't have it, so they suggested a way for him to pay the seller back. He refused to discuss it so he didn't even know what they were suggesting."

"Mr. Madrigal's statement coincides with what you've just said," Bowman stated.

"Later, they pressured Troy into agreeing by threatening his daughter and mine. A car almost drove them off the side of a cliff, as you well know, Summers," Fallon said with a nod toward Alex.

"Yes," Bowman said. "We were lucky he was there and got the license plate."

"Well, you probably won't be able to trace them to a man named Louis Ferone, but I'd almost bet he's behind it. He's the dealer Troy used, and I don't doubt he sent the men to meet with Troy."

"You know Ferone?" Bowman asked.

"I've been very careful not to know him. On the surface, he seems legitimate, but he's been involved in too many mysterious operations for my taste, although nothing has ever been proven out in the open. Still, enough rumors exist to convince me he's not on the up and up. If I'd known Troy was going to use his services, I would have advised against it."

"Do you know who did suggest him?"

"You'll have to ask Troy. All I know is after our mail clerk disappeared, Brett found discrepancies in some shipments…unmarked crates we couldn't identify. I realized immediately that our mail department had been used as a conduit for the Chaco pottery circulating on the black market."

"You know about that?"

"Of course. It's my job to know what's being sold and where, so I pay sources to keep me informed."

"Sounds like we need to know your sources."

"If I revealed them, no one would talk to me. Besides," Fallon said with a smile, "I only deal in information, not goods. A lot of what is told to me is just hearsay, not fact, but I still pay. When I saw those crates, I knew the info on the pottery was true."

"It doesn't make sense. If they had your mail clerk on their payroll and it was so easy to slip the pottery through his department without your knowledge, why did they need Troy's buy-in?"

"I should think it's obvious, Agent Bowman. They wanted to implicate Fallon Enterprises in the crime. They needed someone in management involved to make it viable."

Fallon's conclusion was the same one Alex had come to. Nothing else made sense. The anonymous tip. The shipping manifests and crates left right out in the open. It was all too easy, too obvious. The system would be easily discovered and exposed. It was not a long-term covert operation. Someone had spent a lot of time and money to implicate and drag Fallon Enterprises into the scheme.

"So, Mr. Fallon, do you have a lot of enemies?" Bowman's tone was full of irony.

"Unfortunately, I have many competitors who would love to see my company go under."

"Any of them with Southwest connections?"

"One," Fallon said with a shake of his head. "It always amused me that Rupert Townsend had such a superior attitude when his family's fortune came from robbing Indian graves. His grandfather was an expert at finding and pillaging Chaco sites before the 1906 Antiquities Act protected them. Some say his grandfather never stopped, just went underground, but Rupert always denied it."

"Does this Townsend have a grudge against you?"

"Rupert Townsend would like nothing better than to destroy me and take credit for saving my wife's school." Fallon gave a small laugh. "In fact, I'd bet it's his life's ambition."

Bowman gestured to one of the men standing at the back of the room. "Get Townsend's address and send a car out there. We need to talk to him."

"I doubt you'll have any luck. He probably

already knows his scheme has failed. My daughter said he was supposed to attend the event last night but he never showed, and Townsend owns a jet and homes in half the countries of the world. I doubt you'll ever find him." Fallon gave a rueful shake of his head.

Fallon's statement puzzled Alex. He'd known Townsend had a grudge against Fallon. But would Townsend go to such lengths? If so, somehow, someway, Townsend and his group had been tipped off. The plot unraveled, the mail clerk disappeared and everyone scattered long before Agent Bowman and company could take action...and all because Alex insisted they wait.

Bowman posed more questions to Fallon, about his security company's past experience, the camera system located outside the residence but not inside, and asked if Fallon knew information about private collectors seeking instruments such as La Guitarra.

Fallon shook his head. "I wracked my brain and I can't think of any relevant information. In fact, I can't find any connection whatsoever between my company and La Guitarra. I have no idea who could be behind this or why they did it—and certainly not how."

The weight that had settled in Alex's stomach sank even lower. The helpless, hopelessness of Fallon's tone mirrored his own feelings...and time was running out.

Soon, La Guitarra would be lost forever.

15

Lara spent several fruitless hours trying to rest. She dozed off and on and prayed continuously. Still her mind ran in a vicious little circle.

Alex had used her to get information about her family.

Why didn't he tell her Fallon Enterprises was under investigation? They could have followed all of these suspicious trails and resolved this long ago.

He didn't trust her…yet he'd demanded she trust him and talked about their true selves and her "awakening" as if it were a special gift to him.

Even now, she could hear his voice when he left her in front of the school. "Promise me, Lara, no matter what happens, you'll remember these last few days have meant more to me…"

She wanted to believe…wanted to keep her promise.

Bowman was right. If they'd called off the ceremony, La Guitarra might still be here.

But still…Alex lied.

After a sleepless hour, she'd had enough. What she needed was a workout. She dressed in tights and a leotard. She threw on a filmy skirt, slid into a pair of loose shoes, and grabbed her sweater. Her father had returned just an hour ago so she slipped through the guesthouse as quietly as possible, hoping not to wake him.

The air was still crisp with an early morning chill and the grounds were quiet. No servants moved about. The I.C.E. cars stood empty and still. It was as if everyone and everything—even nature—waited, held its breath for what might come next.

Lara shuddered. She was surprised to see someone walking toward her from the main house carrying a guitar case. Carlos. Last night's news that he and Alex had severed their partnership had come as a shock. Something about his vehement outburst about La Guitarra and his obvious resentment had given her the feeling Carlos believed Alex had somehow caused this tragedy. Did he feel betrayed too? The question poised on the tip of her lips.

He paused on the pathway, awkwardly silent. At last, he gestured to the guitar case. "Christy and I were to have a lesson this morning. I thought it might help to pass the time since I am not allowed to leave." He glanced back at the house. "But she is still asleep. Perhaps later." He gave a half smile, and then continued on his way.

Was this how it was going to be? All of them awkward, suspicious, waiting for something else to happen?

They'd been interviewed privately and were given no information. She didn't know why the I.C.E. was investigating Fallon Enterprises or what connection it had to La Guitarra. Throughout the evening her father had been calm, confident. He knew more than he had told her and she was certain, when he woke, he'd share with her what he could. Maybe then, some of these strange, uncomfortable feelings would ease. In the meantime, she needed a workout to push aside her disquiet.

She entered the main house. Agent Bowman's voice came from the room to the right. Several of the I.C.E. men were in there, too. Alex was seated close to the door. He looked exhausted. Red rimmed his eyes. Dark stubble covered his jaw, and he rested his head in his hand as if he could barely hold it up. Life sparked in his gaze as she crossed the entryway, his expression hopeful, alive.

Lara turned her head and hurried up the stairs. As soon as she closed the dance room door, she sighed in relief. Everything was as it should be. Christy's guitar rested on its stand with the empty case on the floor beside it. The disc player and several CDs were close by. Sunshine poured into the room from the large windows and dust motes floated in the air.

Lara needed the peace. Throwing off her sweater and skirt, she jumped into her stretch routine. Her stressed muscles were tight and cramped. A twenty-minute warm up didn't do enough so she launched into another. No matter how hard she worked, she couldn't get Alex's wounded, hopeful look from her mind.

"Promise me, Lara, no matter what happens, you'll remember…"

How would she ever forget that tortured look? Alex was suffering. Was it from the loss of his guitar or the loss of her trust?

Alex said he couldn't reveal his purpose. No matter what his feelings for her were, he had a duty to perform. But how much truth had he spoken? How much had he used her attraction to him to get information?

"Promise me, Lara, no matter what happens, you'll remember these last few days have meant more to me…"

Was it true?

If not, would he have worked so hard to make things right with the school? Would he have stalled the investigation for the last ceremony? Would he have looked at her with such hope in his gaze?

Why couldn't she get him out of her mind? Music. What she needed was music to dance him away. She pressed the button on the CD player and hurried back into position. As she straightened her back and lifted her shoulders, the strums of Alex's guitar drifted over the air. Flamenco music immediately gripped her soul.

Oh, no. Not that!

Lara lunged across the floor to punch the off button. Her foot accidently kicked the empty guitar case. The notes dropped out of the air and she grasped her stinging toe as something registered. She'd stubbed her toe on the case hard enough to hurt, but the case had not budged. Puzzled, she bent and lifted the case with her fingertips. Heavy. Not empty.

Heart pounding, she flipped the silver snaps and lifted the lid to reveal a round, polished-to-perfection guitar. If she was not mistaken the one Carlos played in their performances.

His guitar was here...so what had he carried away from the house?

~*~

Alex was exhausted and numb, had been numb since La Guitarra disappeared.

Whatever he'd expected, the theft of his guitar was a shock. It made no sense...had no connection with the scheme to implicate Fallon in a black market trade. No matter how he turned it, the theft of La Guitarra had to be a totally separate crime.

"However we look at it, the last person to touch the guitar was Carlos." Bowman stood at the front. A team still scoured the guitar room for fingerprints and evidence. But most of Bowman's immediate team surrounded Alex. Seated in chairs, they seemed as exhausted as he. Even Bowman's shoulders drooped as he covered the information one more time.

"By the book, the last person at the scene has to be our first suspect." Bowman rubbed a hand around the back of his neck.

"But McGraff was with Carlos the whole time. He watched him place the guitar on its stand. Then they locked the door," Alex said.

Bowman was silent for a moment. "Yes, but they came back and opened the doors again. What if 'they' didn't lock it? What if Carlos locked it and with the cloth wrapped around his bleeding hand, managed to switch the keys?"

The men in the room straightened, considering the possibilities.

"He could have had a key similar to the original and McGraff wouldn't have known the difference," Altman, Bowman's second in command, agreed.

Bowman nodded. "Then while McGraff was checking out the thermostat and the power, Bertoleo opened the door, switched the guitars and locked up again. Then he fetched Mike to open the doors one last time so he'd have the perfect alibi."

"But Bertoleo had the original key. If Mike tried to open the door, he would have discovered his was not the right one," Altman said.

Alex shook his head. "All Carlos had to do was reach for the key again. Mike wouldn't hesitate to allow him to open the door. Carlos is above suspicion…or he was before everyone discovered I fired him."

Bowman studied him for a moment. "Does that mean you no longer trust Bertoleo?"

"He has a motive for stealing La Guitarra. Vengeance is a powerful motivator. I can't think of any other reason."

"Money is just as powerful, my friend," Bowman said. "We were about to break up the pottery scheme. Maybe the perpetrators decided La Guitarra was good enough compensation."

Altman nodded his head. "Besides, we searched all of Bertoleo cases and we went over your guesthouse with a microscope. There's no way he hid the guitar there."

Bowman was silent for another moment. "Perhaps, when he made the switch, he hid it here, somewhere in this house."

The men looked at each other.

"We searched this house, too." Altman's tone was dismissive.

"But there's a lot more hiding places here," another man said. "What could it hurt to search again?"

The new thread energized the group.

"Let's get Mike in here again," Bowman said. "I want to know exactly who opened the door and if Carlos could have switched the keys. Then we'll do another sweep of the house."

Lara rushed into the room so fast her flimsy skirt flowed around her. Her face was pale, washed out. Her wide gaze sought Alex.

"Can…can I speak to you alone?"

Her voice brought energy back into his lethargic limbs. She was here, talking to him. That had to be a good sign. He rose to his feet and followed her out. "Lara, I'm so sorry. I…"

"Can we talk about this later? Right now I need to show you something." She took his hand and hurried to the stairs. As she took them two at a time she said, "I didn't want to say anything in front of Agent Bowman and his men. I could be wrong…I don't know. I just…" She was breathless, shook up.

"Slow down. You're not making any sense."

She tugged him inside the dance room and closed the door. "I saw Carlos a while ago, leaving the house with his guitar case. He said he was supposed to have a lesson with Christy this morning. But it's not true. Christy always has lessons at eight. All of her other activities start at ten. He lied, and I didn't realize it until I saw this."

She lifted the lid of Christy's empty guitar case.

"Am I right?" she breathed. "Is this Carlos's guitar?"

Alex could only nod. "How long ago did you see him?"

"Twenty minutes…no. Longer. I'm so sorry, Alex. It had to be almost thirty minutes."

Alex's pulse leapt. Long enough to get away!

He spun and hurried down the back stairs. The foot of the stairs stopped near the kitchen and the back door, closer to the guesthouse. He ran across the compound, heart pumping, weary legs burning. To his relief, his small sports car was parked in its usual place. He burst through the front door into an empty living room. He raced up the stairs, slamming through bedrooms and closet doors. Carlos was nowhere to be found. All of his guitars cases were there except one.

Alex ran back downstairs. "He's gone," he told Lara. The car keys were still on the sideboard and he touched them, his mind racing. "He didn't take my car, so where did he go and how does he plan to get away?"

His gaze landed on the sliding glass door. Immediately a shadowy image flashed in his mind. Carlos had been walking in the forest behind the guesthouse. He'd returned that day just in time to hear Alex's conversation with Bowman. They had their fight, and Alex fired him. Shortly after, Chang disappeared. And Rupert Townsend hadn't shown up, either.

Carlos tipped Chang and Ferone off. Did he do it to get back at Alex? Was payment for Carlos's tip-off their help to spirit La Guitarra away? It had to be the answer.

Alex ran to the glass door. "Do you know what's on the other side of those trees?"

"I think the main road loops back around below."

Fear leapt into Alex's throat. He flung open the door and charged into the scrub pine forest.

"Alex, wait!"

He didn't stop. The pines and bushes were thicker than they seemed but he found what he was looking for. A man's footprints leading down the mountain. He followed them.

The ground sloped steeply. It took all of Alex's concentration to keep progressing as he wove in and out of bushes and trees. He dug his feet into the soft earth for better purchase, doing a half hop down the slope. He could hear Lara behind him. He wanted to shout back at her to stop and go back, but he couldn't spare the time, or the breath. He could hear the cars. He broke out of the trees onto the main road.

No sign of Carlos in either direction. He bent over his knees in frustration, panting.

Lara ran out of the trees to stand beside him, gasping for breath. "Now what?"

"I don't know. I just don't..." An idea came to him. He rose and grasped her arms.

"Listen carefully. Remember the small café just down the road?"

Lara nodded, barely able to catch her breath

"Someone has to be helping Carlos and if a car was waiting for him, it would most likely be there. I'll see if I can catch him. I want you to go back up the hill and get Bowman and his men. Have them meet me at the café. And hurry, Lara."

She nodded again and turned, but Alex caught her arm and pulled her back. He kissed her quick on the lips, spun, and ran down the road.

16

Lara lifted her skirt hem, tucked it into her waistband, and ran back to the trees. Climbing uphill was much harder than going down in the loose soil. She slipped. The soil clung to her leggings and slid into her shoes. She fell forward several times and climbed hand over foot until she could stand, never slowing. She reached the top completely out of breath and still had to cross the compound.

Thinking quickly, she ran into the guesthouse through the still-open glass door, grabbed the keys Alex had fingered moments ago and slid into his car. The engine of his sleek little sports car turned over easily.

Lara gunned the gas pedal to cross the compound in a matter of seconds. She pulled into the driveway by the front door and hit the brakes and the horn at the same time.

The instant one of the men poked his head out the door, she shouted, "Carlos escaped through the forest. Alex followed him to the café on the main road. We'll meet you there!" Then she stomped on the pedal again. The little car shot out of the drive, spewing gravel behind. Lara bumped down the road so fast, she slid into the main road at the base of the hill.

Skidding to a halt, she looked up to see oncoming traffic headed straight for her. With a little exclamation, she threw the gearshift into reverse, managing to back out of the way just in time. She released her breath, counted to two, gunned the accelerator again and caught up with the cars that had just passed her.

Arriving at the café, she spotted Alex in the parking lot by the edge of the road. She screeched to a halt beside him, and he ran around to the driver's side.

"Scoot over."

"What's going on? Did you see him?"

"The owner of the café said a man with a guitar case got into a blue foreign luxury sedan."

"If we know what kind of car we're looking for, why don't we just let Bowman and his men do their work?"

"There's an old airstrip about four miles around the mountain on the outskirts of town." Alex hit the blacktop, already topping the speed limit. "Your father said Townsend has a jet."

"Townsend? Rupert Townsend has something to do with this?"

"I'll explain, but first I need you to call Bowman and tell him what we're doing."

Lara gave Bowman the information, and then listened as the agent told her—loudly and in no uncertain terms—to make Alex stop.

"You tell him." She held the phone away from her ear in Alex's direction.

"What do you think you're doing?" Bowman's voice reverberated.

Alex's tone rose in response. "I'm hoping that if we're too late, I can at least get a glimpse of the plane. Make sure it's Townsend's. Maybe get some numbers off the tail so we can trace it."

Bowman kept yelling but Alex motioned Lara to

hang up.

"What if you're wrong? What if Carlos isn't headed to the airstrip?"

"Then Bowman and his people have a description of the car and it'll be our only hope of finding La Guitarra."

Lost. That priceless instrument would be lost. Its beauty and history would disappear. The knowledge sank deep into Lara's heart, giving their pursuit a new sense of desperation.

Alex turned onto the main road and drove even faster in the twists and turns of the canyon. He gave Lara an abbreviated version of the facts.

At the base of the hill they came upon a crossroad.

Alex hesitated before turning swiftly left. "I hope I got the café owner's directions right."

Lara searched the glove compartment and the side pockets.

"What are you doing?"

"It's a rental, right? Don't they usually have maps of the area?" She found no maps, no highlighted tourist info, nothing.

They sped along the empty road, skirting the edge of the mountains. The road dropped and rose like a roller coaster. As they crested a small hill, another vehicle topped a distant one.

"Alex, look! Is that car blue?"

They went below the hill before they could get a good look.

"I couldn't tell for sure. The mountain's shadow makes everything dark."

He notched up the speed. The car hit the rolling hills almost at a bounce before the road straightened and then fell into the valley below. They came up the last hill.

Lara looked across the open plain. In the distance, she saw the gleaming white lines of a jet parked on a runway cut out of desert brush.

"It *is* them! There's the jet."

The road had leveled by now, and they could see the car a few miles ahead. Alex jammed the accelerator to the floor, and the vehicle leapt forward. "We should be able to catch them. This car has a powerful engine."

The speedometer inched up the numbers. Seventy-five. Eighty.

Lara closed her eyes at ninety.

The blue car was just ahead of them. It accelerated, putting more distance between them.

The sports car's engine roared, and the miles between them disappeared.

Lara held her breath as they sped within two car lengths of the blue sedan. Two people were in the car—a driver and, on the passenger's side, Carlos.

Alex veered into the lane of oncoming traffic.

"What are you doing?" Lara clutched the dash.

"I'm going to get ahead of them and force them to slow down. It'll give Bowman and his people time to catch up."

"Are you crazy? What if cars come down the road?"

"We had a good view of the road from the hill. As far as I could see, it's empty. I'll watch for cars. You keep an eye on Carlos and his partner."

Lara gritted her teeth and tightened her grip on the dash. As they inched closer, Carlos's white, strained face came into view. He appeared to be shouting at the driver. Lara was almost level with the driver. Their gazes met just before he lifted a gun and pointed it straight at her.

"A gun, Alex! He has a gun!"

Alex hit the brakes and the sports car jerked hard. The sedan shot ahead as their vehicle shook and twisted, trying to swerve out of control. Alex wrestled with the wheel as he let up on the brakes. The swerving stopped, and they coasted to a stop in the middle of the road.

In the sudden silence, Lara could hear her own gasping breath.

Alex gripped her hand. "Are you all right?"

"Yes, but they're getting away."

"Let them. I'm not risking your life, even for La Guitarra." He wrapped his hand around her neck and tugged her toward him. He was leaning in to kiss her, when the sound of skidding brakes drew their attention.

The brake lights on the vehicle ahead lit and it screeched to a halt. The back-up lights flared as the car started backing up.

"What are they doing? I'm letting them go."

Something clicked with Lara. "They're coming back."

"Why? They could be on the plane and out of here before Bowman arrives."

"Because I recognized the driver," Lara said in a calm quiet voice. "He's a dealer, and I've met him before. His name is Louis Ferone."

"Your father suspected he might be connected, but we had no proof." Alex's expression hardened and he jerked into action, slamming the car into gear. He couldn't turn the car around without the risk of getting stuck in the sandy shoulders, so he slammed the gearshift again. The car bucked backwards. With his arm looped over the seat, Alex backed down the road at a high speed.

The getaway car was gaining on them, coming fast.

Reaching a spot in the road where the dirt was packed, Alex slammed to a brief stop, then whipped into a three-point turn and gunned the gas. They were headed in the right direction, but they'd lost precious time.

The sedan caught up to them and rammed their tail end.

Alex wrestled with the wheel, trying to keep control. "I just need a few seconds. This car will outrun them if I can just get a little distance." Even as he spoke, there was a loud pop, and then another.

"What's that?" Lara turned back.

"Gunfire! He's shooting. Get down!"

Lara ducked her head just as another, larger explosion rocked the car, a violent rattling vibration.

"He hit a tire. Hang on!"

The car hit the loose dirt and slid off the road.

Lara screamed as it spun in circles.

Alex whipped the wheel, turning into the spinout. The car rattled to a halt.

Lara almost sobbed with relief.

Alex reached across her and opened the door. "Get out, Lara. Slide out and stay down."

With their heads ducked, they faced each other across the front seat. Alex's features were grim and she understood in an instant. She could identify Louis Ferone. He wouldn't let her escape.

Lying flat, Alex jerked open the glove compartment and rifled through it.

Lara punched the button on her seat belt and slid

backwards to a crouch outside the car.

Alex touched something beneath his seat and the trunk sprang open. Then he climbed out beside her.

Dirt swirled around them in a dusty cloud. Keeping the sports car as cover, Alex pushed Lara down the length of the car. At the back, he raised his head high enough to peek inside the trunk. He pulled out a tire iron and handed it to her. Then he grabbed two flares.

The blue sedan screeched to a halt behind the dust cloud.

"Listen carefully." Alex kept his voice low, his gaze fixed. "When we see him, watch the direction he takes. If he comes to the front of the car, you go around to the other side. Keep your head down and wait. I'll draw him off."

"What do you mean 'draw him off'?" she whispered.

"I'm going to distract him so you can get behind him."

"You'll be a target, Alex. He'll kill you."

"The minute he gets a clear shot at me, I'll light the flares in his face. He'll be momentarily blinded. It will give you time to hit him. Keep your eyes turned away from the flare and don't miss. Hit him hard enough to knock him out. And Lara—don't leave your back to the road. Carlos might decide to follow him."

Lara nodded and swallowed hard.

"If he comes around to the back, you go the opposite direction. Understand?"

Lara didn't have time to answer.

Ferone appeared out of the dust, both hands gripping a gun pointed in front of him. He paused long enough to get a good look at the car. Then he strode toward the front.

Alex shoved her around to the left.

Crouching low, Lara ran down the side of the car. She'd reached the front fender when she heard the fizzle of a flare coming to life. Bright light flashed under the car and all around her.

Lara stood and looked up to see the gun pointed straight at her. She gasped.

The gunman's eyes narrow with intent.

A bright, burning flare catapulted through the air and struck Ferone in the side of the head. He yelped with pain and ducked. In the next instant, Alex flew over the hood, diving for Ferone. He struck the man, and they both flew backward.

They hit the ground with loud grunts. The gun skittered across the dirt, yards away from Lara.

Alex and Ferone rolled once, twice across the dirt.

Lara moved forward to grab the gun.

Carlos appeared out of the dust headed for the gun, too.

The tire iron was still in Lara's hand. She gripped it. Filled with righteous fury, she ran toward Carlos, the iron held above her head.

One moment his gaze was fixed on the gun. The next, it turned toward Lara. He shouted in surprise and threw up an arm.

Lara slammed the iron straight down.

The makeshift weapon struck a glancing blow to his head. Stunned, Carlos fell backwards to the ground.

Lara spun around, ready to help Alex.

He straddled the gunman. Alex let go of Ferone's shirt. The man slumped to the side. For a moment, the only sound was Alex's tortured breathing.

A siren echoed over the hills.

As Alex rose to his feet, Lara tossed the tire iron and ran to him.

He wrapped his arms around her. "I thought I'd lost you." He murmured as he buried his face in her hair.

A small nervous laugh escaped. "I thought so, too!"

"You were almost killed." He cupped her chin, his long, graceful fingers scraped and bloodied. "I don't know what I would have done if something had happened to you, Lara."

Dirt streaked his cheek and went into a nasty scrape just beneath his right eye. She reached for it, but he caught her hand and pressed her fingertips to his chest.

"Lara, I love you." The words were barely said when a car skidded to a stop in the middle of the road.

"I believe you," she whispered, and touched his cheek as Bowman, gun drawn, ran toward them.

"Just what did you two think you were doing?"

With one arm wrapped around Lara's waist, Alex faced the angry agent. "It was my fault. I dragged Lara into this and almost got her killed."

"Hey, I followed you," Lara said. "I wasn't about to let you have all the fun."

Alex didn't laugh. "Trust me. There was nothing fun about seeing a gun pointed at you."

"My first adventure," she said in low voice. "Another first with you...and I hope not the last."

Lara's doubts disappeared. He'd risked his life to save hers. She no longer doubted his love or his good intentions. Other things needed to be discussed, many more explanations between them, but Lara acknowledged Alex's love for her and she loved him.

One of Bowman's men carried a guitar case he'd retrieved from the back of the blue car.

Alex released Lara long enough to look inside and confirm it was La Guitarra.

Bowman slammed the cover shut and barked orders. "You two stay here, out of trouble. Altman, you come with me. The jet is taxiing down the runway. We can't stop it, but maybe we can get close enough to get some identifying information."

"I'm sure it belongs to Townsend," Lara said.

Bowman paused.

She gestured to the gunman still unconscious on the ground. "That's why he tried to kill us. I recognized him. His name is Louis Ferone. He's an antiquities dealer and Troy told me Rupert Townsend gave Ferone his recommendation. I'm sure Townsend's on the jet."

Alex and Bowman exchanged glances.

"You'd better hurry, though," she said. "If you give Townsend enough time, he'll come up with an alibi or find political sanctuary. Extraditing him could become impossible."

Another car showed up. An ambulance wailed in the distance. Sirens echoed in the hills around them.

Suddenly, Lara just wanted to go home.

Bowman conferred with an Arizona patrolman, and then came back to them. "We can wrap up here. You two go back to the house and stay put. Don't pull any more hair-raising stunts like this one or I'll put you under house arrest."

"Don't worry." Alex wrapped his arm around Lara. "I won't allow anything else to happen to her."

She and Alex climbed into the police car.

Alex pulled her closer, almost as if he were afraid to be separated from her.

Lara loved the feeling. Easing her head back, she closed her eyes. In what seemed like a very short time, they arrived at the house.

Her father hurried out.

Lara ran into his arms.

"What were you thinking? You had no business following those men."

"It's my fault, sir. I take full responsibility." Alex spoke from behind Lara. "If I'd known Ferone was in the car and Lara knew him, I'd never have risked her life."

"Risked her life? Ferone attacked you?"

Lara could feel her father's muscles bunching in tension. "Don't you think you've done enough to my daughter? I know she has feelings for you and you used those feelings. Did you have to risk her life, as well?"

Alex hung his head, didn't even try to argue.

Did he feel he deserved punishment? Was he so guilt-ridden he'd take her father's public chastisement? Would he go even further, would he profess a love he didn't really feel? Were the feelings she was certain of before simply an emotional reaction to their danger?

Alex's willingness to save her was genuine, but she also understood him well enough to know he would risk his life to save anyone. He would see it as his duty...the same duty that kept him silent while he completed his investigation. Alex was a man of duty and honor. An honorable man would be determined to do right by her even if he didn't love her. Minutes before, she was convinced of Alex's feelings for her. Now she doubted again. Why didn't she know her own mind?

Milly's words floated back at her. *Maybe if you know the Lord's plan for you, then you can trust your own heart.*

Her father took a deep breath, preparing to lash out at Alex again.

"Dad," Lara said. "Dad." This time she spoke louder.

Her father paused and turned his gaze toward her.

"I appreciate your concern, Dad...I do. But whatever is between Alex and me, it's up to us to resolve it, don't you think?"

Taken aback, her father blinked. Then his posture wilted. "Yes. Yes, I should leave it in your capable hands."

She turned back to Alex. "Will you walk with me to the pool?"

Alex nodded.

Her father gripped both of her hands. "Lara," he spoke softly, for her ears only. "When this is settled, I'd like you to come back to New York with me. I want to take some time off to spend with you. We have a lot to talk about."

"I'd like that, Dad. It sounds wonderful."

Alex waited for her at the pool. The water sparkled as it flowed over the infinity edge. The canyon sprawled out before them, rolling into the plain below. Just looking at the rippling waves gave Lara a measure of peace.

Alex looked as troubled, as guilty, as he had when her father flung accusations at him.

"You didn't have to stand there and take my father's criticism," she said in a low voice.

"Yes, I did. It was my fault."

"Yes," she whispered. "I guess you would think that."

Alex studied her. "What happened out there on the road, Lara, didn't change my feelings. It convinced me even more of my love for you." Alex sensed her doubt and grasped her, pulling her into his arms. "I'm expected in Madrid in two days. I have to get on a plane tomorrow. Come with me, Lara. Marry me." He held her closer, murmured in her ear. "I have a villa on the outskirts of Madrid. It's been in my mother's family for generations. There's a courtyard and a fountain surrounded by orange trees. In the evening, we can sit by the fountain while the scent of orange blossoms fills the air. You'd like that, wouldn't you?"

Lara nodded. New York. Spain. The two men she loved most devoting their time to her. A wonderful dream come true.

So why did she feel such a disquiet? Why did the images of those two places seem so wrong? If she didn't want to be with her father or Alex, where did she want to be?

"I promise, Lara, the sunsets in Spain are as spectacular as the ones in Sedona."

Unbidden, an image came to her. A cliff. Red rocks below. In the distance, the sun set in an orange sky of fire. On the plain, cars sparkled like diamonds.

Lara knew where she wanted to be.

Once again, Alex had suspected, had known the secrets of her heart even before she did. Smiling, she stepped out of his embrace.

"You know where I need to be, don't you?"

He tried to pull her back. She shook her head. "No, Alex. From the beginning, you've told me to be true to myself. You were right. For the first time in my life, I'm going to find my path, where I belong."

He started to protest, but she pressed two fingers to his lips. "Don't try to change my mind or convince me, Alex. You might actually succeed because you're so very good at it. But if you love me as much as you say, you'll let me find out where the Lord wants me to be. You'll leave me, go home, and do the same for yourself. When you know that, and if you still want me, you'll know where to find me." Standing on her toes, she kissed where moments ago her fingers had touched. Then she turned and walked back to the house.

Epilogue

Lara crawled up and over the cliff. Rising to her feet, she brushed the dirt off her hands and jeans. Easing her body to the ground, she sat, flopped her legs over the edge, and released a deep sigh. Every day after she completed her work, she climbed the cliff for a workout, and then sat and watched the sun set.

Soon, it would be too hot to climb. June was just around the corner. The summer months would be busy as they prepared for the school's opening in the fall. So much had happened, not just for the school, but also for her family.

These last months had been the most rewarding of her life. Only a few things were missing.

Feeling he had failed, Brett resigned his position. No matter how hard her father protested, Brett insisted he'd lost his sense of purpose and direction and needed time off. Determined to find himself, he packed his things in boxes, loaded them into the back of his black Porsche, and drove into the sunset. He was headed to Santa Fe, New Mexico.

Lara missed her best friend, but she understood.

She finally convinced her father she was staying in Sedona, so he offered her Brett's position. Instead of returning to New York, he spent a month with Lara, helping her settle into her new job. They talked and laughed and remembered. It was one of the happiest times Lara had ever experienced with her father, and the time together gave her an even greater sense of purpose and confidence.

A popular architectural magazine interviewed Troy. As soon as the full-page picture spread appeared, their home was nominated by the magazine and won the honor of "best of the year." After that, design offers and requests for consultations poured in. The extra money helped pay off Troy's debts.

Eliza was able to scale back her work schedule. She and Troy had decided to adopt another child.

Christy had joined a horseback riding club and made some new friends, but she was especially close to one cocky young cowboy/race car driver. And no matter how busy her new friends kept her, she declared she would have plenty of time to be a good big sister.

A long black limo drove into the parking lot below. Milly and Avery climbed out. Milly paused, turned, and waved up at Lara.

Lara waved back, closed her eyes and lifted her face to catch the last bright rays of the sun.

Her mother's dream. Her father's money. Lara's vision. It had taken all three for the Fallon School of Art to take shape.

Milly and Avery had dedicated the funds to build dormitories and small bungalows for the families of underprivileged children. They'd broken ground on the buildings last month and every day they were in town, Milly and Avery drove out to see the progress.

Business Solutions, the computer company, created an endowment for scholarships and Dr. Jerome's curriculum was in place.

All the school needed now was to choose a director of education. Lara had received applications from many sources and from all over the world...except from the one place she wanted to see. She'd hoped she'd find one from Madrid. But none had come.

The past months had shown her what she could do, what she was meant to do. Below her was the evidence of what God had planned for her, and it was good.

She found her new life rewarding but not complete. She missed Alex, and hoped he missed her, but as the months passed with no word, she began to feel her suspicions were true.

Alex's feelings for her had been based more on duty than love.

They hadn't spoken since the day they said good-bye at the airport. Their last kiss had been tender, sweet...bittersweet. It seemed their love, like Juan's and Luisa's, was not meant to be.

She avoided any reminder of him. She could not listen to his music...nor any Flamenco music. She rarely danced. But she couldn't stop coming here. Sometimes as she sat on the edge of the world to watch the sunset, she'd close her eyes and hear the haunting strains of a gypsy song and smell the smoke of a campfire.

Today she heard footsteps and turned.

Alex strode across the cliff top.

She blinked several times, not certain he was real. She started to jump up, but he was already beside her, easing down, his long legs slipping over the edge. Lara was speechless, motionless. She couldn't take her eyes off him.

The setting sun touched his skin with a golden glow. His hair was shorter, his dark eyes alive with humor and pleasure.

Finally, she touched his cheek to make sure he was real.

He grasped her fingers and kissed them.

"How...how did you get here? I didn't see a car."

"I rode up with Milly and Avery. They dropped me off where the fire lane meets the road."

Below, Milly and Avery stood hand in hand. Milly gave Lara another small wave, and then they walked back to their limo.

"It's obvious you found your purpose. This is amazing, Lara." Alex gestured to the grounds.

Lara smiled, devouring the sight of him. His beautiful, long fingers grasping her hand. His firm jaw. The full lips with a little tilt on one side.

"What about you?" she murmured. "Did you find your purpose?"

"Well, I've resigned. I wanted to fill out paperwork for a new position, but I preferred to apply in person."

Lara's heart leapt, and she cupped his face with her hands. Oh, how she loved that smile. She wanted to kiss it, to cover it with her mouth, but his words were too important. She needed to hear them. "What about your work with UNESCO?"

"Now that everyone knows about my work, I'm not as valuable to them. I doubt I'll be doing any more investigations."

This time, she couldn't stop herself, she kissed him, covering his delicious half-smile with her lips. A thought occurred to her, and she pulled back slightly. "What about your villa?"

"It's been there for generations, Lara. It's not going anywhere. It will be there when we're ready."

Lara smiled. "We?"

"Absolutely. I learned exactly where I'm supposed to be. By your side. Watching you. Waiting for your next awakening."

She gave a little laugh. "I don't think there'll be many more of those."

Alex threaded his fingers through her hair. "Oh yes, there'll be many more, sweetheart," he murmured. "I can't wait to see your face the first time you hold our child in your arms. I want to watch you cry as I walk our daughters down the aisle and when our sons throw their graduation caps in the air." His voice was so low and tender it sounded like a song. "But most of all, my love, there are sunsets all over the world just waiting for us."

Lara needed to hear nothing more. She wrapped her arms around his neck and pressed her lips to his.

Free Book Offer

We're looking for booklovers like you to partner with us! Join our team of influencers today and receive at least one free eBook per month. Maybe more!

For more information
Visit http://pelicanbookgroup.com/booklovers
or e-mail
booklovers@pelicanbookgroup.com

www.ingramcontent.com/pod-product-compliance
Lightning Source LLC
Chambersburg PA
CBHW030107260626
47156CB00008B/2557